DIMMER

-NIGHT HUNT-

DIMMER

-NIGHT HUNT-

ROBERT F. JONES

ASA PUBLISHING CORPORATION

AN INNOVATIVE OUTSOURCE BOOK PUBLISHING HYBRID

ASA Publishing Corporation
29 S. Monroe St., Ste. 201, Monroe, Mi. 48161
An Accredited Publishing House with the BBB
www.asapublishingcorporation.com

This book was published in the United States of America.
Great State of Michigan

Table of Contents

CHAPTER EIGHTEEN

EPILOGUE

DIMMER

-NIGHT HUNT-

CHAPTER ONE

The Beginning

"The world changes, we do not, therein lies the irony

that kills us."

— Anne Rice, *Interview with the Vampire*

Blood! That was all she saw. Blood of her friends, her comrades in arms. Wait; not just blood but, other, more disturbing things. Things that nature did not intend to be outside the body. An eye out of socket. A guy holding his own liver. A kidney next to a foot. A heart still beating on the grass. The most gruesome to view were entrails coming out of a woman's guts. Jenny looked at all of them, these fallen soldiers, these battle buddies, these corpses she called friends. She should have done more. She should have … she should have … she should have …

Pulling her from her recurring nightmare was the sound of Gloria Estefan singing, *Let it Loose*. It was Friday: Jenny's favorite day of the week. Her eyes went wide. That scene of the bloody field felt so vivid to her. She swore, for a moment, that coppery smell of the blood was still there. She sat up and realized she was in her barracks, on her bunk. Simple frame, simple blue mattress, covered by a sheet. A chest of drawers on one side, a smaller coffee table drawer near the tiny walk in closet where she stored the majority of her military gear. The familiarity of it calmed her and reminded her that she was back in the real world. The nightmare, buried behind conscious thought, was now starting to feel like a distant, long forgotten experience that had happened to stranger.

It was always the same dream, the day after her period ended, and she didn't understand why. The recurring dream was something she had experienced since she was a child. Once she asked her mother what it could mean, but that was a big mistake. The then 13-year old Jenny spent hours being psychoanalyzed by her mother, which culminated in Jenny getting the talk again. She warned her not to have sex until marriage, a promise she kept until she turned 16 and slept with Andrew Gac. He was drummer in one of the dozens of high school rock bands and she broke her promise in the back of his dad's van. After that, she never brought up the dream or anything sexual to her parents. Instead, she did what many teenagers with an overbearing upbringing did; left home and joined the Army.

She realized her alarm, from her iPhone, was still buzzing. She moaned, turned it off, and forced herself out of her bunk. She stood up, while shaking her head, on the way to the bathroom. She hated these mornings: or Army mornings, as she had called them, since she completed basic training. Five days until a field mission and she still had to do PT. Why did she torture herself like this: because Uncle Sam was ultimately going to pay for her dreams.

"I'm a slut for the federal government," she muttered while brushing her hair from her eyes. "They tell me where to go, and what position I go into. Maybe I should have become a stripper. The pay is more and the hours are better."

Turning on her play list, Pat Benatar started singing "Love is a Battlefield". Jenny Dang looked at herself in the mirror. A man who loved her or just saw her on the street would be in awe of her. She was 5 foot 4 with brown eyes, a kind smile, oriental features and skin color due to her Vietnamese heritage. Perfect teeth with dyed, highlighted, brownish hair completed her package. Her slim frame and proportional features would make a man go to his knees, sob, and beg her for affection. But Jenny wasn't interested in a man's affections at this time. She was interested in finishing her remaining six months in the Army then going back to San Francisco, California. She was going to apply to the San Francisco Ballet Company. If not that one, any Ballet company that would take her. For that, she needed school and she needed the money. To get it, she enlisted in the Army to get the Post 911 GI Bill.

Jenny's passion for dancing began when she was only six and her father took her to a show performed by the Vietnam National Opera and Ballet back in California. Her father, a former actor, always loved going to the theater and ballets and would take his wife and daughter with him whenever he could get tickets. When he had gotten these, he only had two, and they were not in the best place to view the show. However, Jenny had never been with him before she was six, he choose to take her instead of his wife, who was playing canasta that night. Jenny remembered how excited he was seeing dancers from his home country. A country, thanks to the war, he hadn't seen in thirty years.

Jenny was being a brat the whole way, struggling in her father's arms, saying, "I don't want to go. I don't want to go."

"It's like going to the movies," cooed her father, stroking her back even as she kicked and screamed. As her father took them to their seats, the excited crowd mostly drowned out her screams. She distinctly remembered her father stubbornly ignoring the others around them. He didn't own a tux back then, working as a cabby, only a used tan sport coat and slacks, making him stand out like a pimple in the crowd.

Then the lights lowered, and the show began, and all of Jenny's whining melted away when the members of the opera and ballet put on Swan Lake. She remembered how graceful the dancers were on those stages, how their bodies seemed to almost create the music, she turned to her father asking if her belief was true.

Her father responded with, "In a way, yes. Hush now, my love. Enjoy."

When it was over several hours later, Jenny clapped her little hands together as hard as she could, watching the stage members grasping hands, and taking a bow.

When they left, Jenny looked up at her father and said, "Dad, when I grow up, I want to be a dancer just like them."

Her father smiled and nodded. It was the beginning of almost twelve years of practice, rehearsals, recitals, and shows. Her parents encouraged this behavior, thinking it was just a good pastime for their daughter, not believing it was a serious career choice.

That changed when she was seventeen and she told them that she wanted to go apply to Julliard's. This wasn't an ideal education path they wanted their daughter to take and they spent two years trying to talk her out of it.

Finally, it all concluded with her father saying that he wasn't going to pay for her to dance forever, and unless she got serious with wanting to go to a proper college, she could kiss her tuition money goodbye. Jenny, eighteen, and angry at this point, left and went to find other options to pay for the schooling. That was until she met a recruiter at her high school and learned that the US

Army would pay for her school. Learning this, and being of age, she joined up when she turned 19, and never looked back. Her parents were furious at her for following her dreams and now she was completely on her own.

That was two and half years ago and she was nearing the crunch time. Six months away from her sweet, sweet freedom, she was already filling and sending out applications to dozens of dance schools across California and New York, and even the other 48 states. At 21, she was still young enough to make a career of her skill in dancing, which, according to her various instructors, was far above the average and nearing the stylings of Anna Pavlova. But as of right now, all she had to worry about was being able to run for at least four miles, go to work, go home, then go to her class for ballet instruction and then enjoy her weekend.

She washed her face, took a quick piss, changed into her winter PTs, which consisted of black jacket, black shorts, long black pants, black cover, black gloves, and black socks. That was a lot of black. Jesus and she thought green was too much with the OCP. The only break with the black was the yellow stripe and Army logo on her jacket and the one on her shorts. She put on her green PT belt, grabbed her key card to get into barracks room, and headed downstairs. She got off the second floor and down to the ground floor, where she passed Sergeant Vidal and Private Snead, who were on CQ for the next three hours, then had the rest of the day off and sleep until Monday. Lucky bastards. Thursday, the best day to have CQ. Guaranteed three-day weekend. The only thing better was a duty on a Tuesday, had Wednesday off, then go into a four-day weekend on Thursday. That was the White Whale of all CQ duties, and one of the few where people paid money to get on to, instead of it being the usual other way around.

Jenny yawned and headed outside into the Autumn air. It was October first, and it was a crisp 42 degrees. Fuck Fort Drum. The cold came too early. She walked about three-fourths of a mile to the PT field, and saw Ojehta, McManah, Jobe, Hamish, and Hickman already there, and including her, six out of the forty people that made up the Third Platoon of the 514 MSC Company.

"Hey," she said to each as she passed them.

"Hey," they said, each having a variation of, 'How's it going?', 'What's up?', or her favorite, 'What you doing tonight?'

Sosa was doing stretches and behind her, Davis. Ten minutes later, Russel. Then Pommings. The mix of single soldiers and married ones, all of whom made their way to the PT field. The field was a large square across the street from the 549 Support battalion. The 549 was Jenny's battalion, and her company, 514 GSC, and she was in Third Platoon, GSE. Their job: fix heaters, generators, water pumps, those kinds of things. It was a good job, and the majority of the time thanks in part to the COVID pandemic, she was able to get off on time. She also enjoyed her Platoon Sergeant, Sergeant First Class Alibudbun, who was a fun and joking Filipino but also good at his job.

While waiting for formation, she was joined by two of her best friends; Specialist Hamish and Specialist Hickman. Hamish was the tallest guy in the platoon, almost 6 foot 4 and the third tallest in the company. He had coarse, short, brown hair, tanned but light skin. He had blue eyes, or ice eyes as he called them. He had a thin frame, which deceptively held a lot of strength within, thanks to the fact he built and farmed for most of his life and he's twenty-three. That body contained a very warm heart and a tenderness Jenny had found in very few men, including her father. A heart that had dreams of being a doctor one day. Hickman, on the other hand, was an African-American New

Yorker through and through. His military faded black hair, his dark eyes, thin frame only a little taller than Jenny herself. His teeth were almost ghostly light in the darkness, and perfect. Hickman was also a guitar player, his heroes being that of the great guitar gods, Jimi Hendrix, Gary Clark Jr., and Robert Randolph, among others of that great pantheon of musicians. He was great player, and even formed a band with a few other soldiers. His dream was to one day become a good enough musician to make a living, but not the average goal of making it big. His dream seemed to have a tinge of reality; his channel on YouTube averaging over 500,000 views per video and he was making descent money from it.

She loved these two guys because, like her, they shot for near impossible dreams for themselves. Dancing, singing, and medicine, these were their wants, the military was the means to obtain it.

"Hey, Dang," said Hickman as he and Hamish walked up.

"Hey boys," Jenny said, giving them her dazzling smile. The two smiled back.

"Ready for the field on Wednesday?" asked Hamish, his calm almost serene voice, giving one the sense he held great wisdom.

"Ready, and already thinking of the screwdriver that I'll be drinking as soon as it is over," she laughed, not missing Hickman's rubbing his forehead and red tint in his eyes. "See you already had a few."

Hickman smiled back, putting a menthol Kool to his lips and lighting it with a zippo, the orange glow of the tip bright in the dark morning at 0615. Speaking in his hip hop Queen's rock star voice, "Hey, girl, if I can't run five miles after having a few belts the night before, I have no business in the Army."

"I think you have a bit of a problem," said Hamish in his old wise man's voice.

"I know I have a problem," said Hickman with a smile, "I just don't want to solve it. Surprised you don't have the problem."

Hamish cracked a grin. "Someone is needed to make sure all of you get home safely after your nights of weekend debauchery."

"Weekend debauchery? What the fuck?" Hickman shook his head, "Man, you'd get your ass kicked in Queens for saying that puritan white boy shit."

Jenny laughed, "What about me?"

Hickman said, "You'd get twenty marriage proposals, at least, in Tiny Little Saigon in Chinatown."

"You're making that up," said Hamish.

"Go check out New York City. Point to any part of the map, I guarantee you'd find a neighborhood there that is an enclave for whatever country you point at."

"I will as soon as the pandemic ends."

Hickman took another puff then their Squad leader came up. At 5 foot 1, Sergeant Camila Garcia always turned heads when she came up the field. She was Columbian, not thin but her body well made with large breasts that bulged under her PTs, along with a nice ass. Her black hair was highlighted with brown streaks, which went perfect with her cocoa skin complexion. Her lips seemed to be designed for kissing. Her nose was also well made and her brown eyes made one drown in their beauty. However, if one was to try to lay a hand on her Latina perfection, they were gonna end up on the ground with a broken arm. Garcia was a soldier, first and foremost. She took care of her people, taught them, kept them motivated, and let them know what the hell was going on, never leaving things last minute. She always made sure to get to know her soldiers and find ways to increase their chances of reaching their goals both inside and outside the military. She found Jenny a ballet instructor who gave her private lessons at her studio, even with the pandemic going on. She founded Hamish online courses he could take to help him get into med school. She managed to find a chaplain who would allow Hickman to use the music equipment to jam on after work and on weekends. She was just that awesome. In return, her soldiers gave her the best they could at work, at Army boards, and even at Army classes. Her team leaders, Sergeant Sengal and Corporal Pag, were also motivators, following their squad leader's example.

The three went to parade rest for her, arms behind back, legs apart, but almost instantly, she snapped, "Relax boys and girl. Ok, where is Sosa and Jackson?"

"Here."

The final two soldiers of Garcia's squad came up. Jackson was twenty-two, a big blonde boy who weighed 259 pounds, and was also on profile because of his leg. Sosa was Caucasian and from Puerto Rico. She was average looking and lived off post with her wife.

Garcia nodded and said, "Good, ok, saw Sengal in his car and Pag over by the bars, so that's all my soldiers. So, who is ready for the weekend?"

"Hooah!" yelled her soldiers, but she gave Hickman a smile.

"Smells like someone already got started," she said. Hickman's mouth went tight, and his face darkened with a blush. Jenny and the others chuckled, and Garcia smiled and said, "Nothing four miles won't be able to sweat out."

Hickman smiled at that. "Yes, Sergeant."

She turned and said, "Lets form up people, First Squad leads."

They lined up and a minute later were joined by Sengal and Pag. Pag was a hair shorter than Hamish, and was hard body, the best PT guy in the squad, and one of the most motivated soldiers despite his rank. He was the only Corporal in the unit, his leadership recognizing his outstanding skills as a leader. Sengal was more laid back. He was from Togo, Africa, soft spoken, but looked out for his guys. Sengal was Jenny's team leader, and she liked him fine. Good guy, with values, and a family. They were all family, brothers and sister slogging their way through the motorpool then going off to live their lives. Garcia was that immovable center. She was both mom and boss.

Sergeant First Class Alibudbun came up at six-twenty, seeing his soldiers already lined up. He was almost fifty, had a bald spot, and his Filipino features were forever in a state of fatherly kindness. He smiled at his platoon and said, "Morning people. Guessing you're already for the weekend, huh?"

"Hooah!" yelled the thirty-two soldiers and NCOs that made up Third Platoon.

After seeing everyone was there, he stood there in front of the platoon, taking jokes and slinging them right back as first, second, and fourth platoon were all finishing up their checks. Then the First Sergeant, First Sergeant Michael, came up. He was short, barely five feet, but the other platoon leaders turned to him, sent up their reports, letting him know who was present and who wasn't, and for what reason. Finally, the horn went off, and upon First Sergeant's orders, Alibudbun called Third Platoon to attention as revelry started, and they saluted the flag. When it was done, he said, again, as instructed by the First Sergeant, "Order arms." Then the platoon went back to attention.

"Company," said the First Sergeant, "take command of your platoons; start PT."

Alibudbun saluted the First Sergeant along with HQ Platoon, Second Platoon, and Forth Platoon leaders, and turned back to his squad, saying, "Squad leaders, take charge, conduct PRT."

SGT Garcia and the other Squad leaders saluted him, he returned it. Once finished, Garcia yelled, "Pag, you lead! Everyone, to the usual spot! Jackson, to profile PT!"

First Squad fell out, and they went to work out until 0800. After PT, they went back to their barracks, and for those who lived off post, their homes, to, as the old Army would say, to shit, shower, and shave. Jenny got to her room first before her roommate, Russel, and was able to shower first. The barracks room had a shared a bathroom and kitchen area, but each soldier had their own bedroom. Jenny shaved her armpits and legs while taking a quick shower. After drying herself, she went into her room and changed into her OCPs and combat boots. She headed to the chow hall, grabbed a to-go plate, and walked to work wearing a mask. Fucking COVID. The only good thing about that whole mess was the last guy getting the boot and the free two-week vacation she got from being forced to stay inside.

She got to work and entered the break room. She ate her eggs and bacon fast, drank her coffee slow, then went to the locker room. When she got there, she changed out of her OCP top, and put on her coveralls she used for work. It was loose fitting, but it worked well to keep her skin oil free, but not her fingernails. Gunk got under them, and before her dance lessons, she always had to clean them out. Madam Roseta abhorred dirty nails, and always told Jenny to take time with her appearance. On the stage, you had to be perfect, as all eyes were on you and the crowd would notice one small flaw.

She then pulled out her cell phone to check the time and saw she had a text message. It was from her mother, asking her to call her when she had time.

Jenny took a breath. She still talked to her mother, but the woman was still trying to get her to stop pursuing her dreams of being a dancer and come home and do something more practical with her life. As if she wasn't trying to do that for years now. For one resentful moment, she thought about not answering. It wouldn't be the first time either. She sighed, deciding to hold off making the call until, or after, lunch and headed out to the GSC shop in the motorpool, where Jackson and Hamish were sitting in their coveralls, ready for work.

She sat next to Hamish, who was reading a letter, his face stony. Hamish was the only person in the world she knew about that still received handwritten letters. She looked at the stony expression on his face, and asked, "Your sister again?"

Though Jackson was too concerned about what was on his phone to care about their conversation, Hamish nodded at her, indicating toward the door as he did so. She nodded back and the two went outside. There was a picnic table and the two sat next to each other, letting Hamish say what he needed to say when he was ready.

Jenny and Hickman were among the handful of people in the unit who knew Hamish was Amish. He lived in an Amish community in Ohio, near a small town called Berlin, one of the largest in the Ohio. He had two sisters and a younger brother, and his mother and father were still alive. Unlike most of his community, Hamish had graduated from high school, despite his father's disapproval. This was due to Hamish's want to know as much as he could, even from the English, as Amish called any who were not Amish. During this time, more and more Amish were being born with genetic defects that were popping up in the growing Amish community. Hamish's brother was born with downs syndrome and was unable to see out of one eye.

Hamish, determined to do something, requested his father to ask the Bishop to allow him to attend college and apply for medical school. He had the grades to get in and his grade point average was over 4.0. His father refused, saying Hamish was needed on the farm and he had to help his brother. They argued and it ended when his father hit him. Hamish, angry, left to go into town, wanting to be alone and away from his dad. He went the library, one of the few Amish to go there regularly, saw a flyer for the US Army recruiting office in Wooster, Ohio. In secret, he made contact with them, and a recruiter met him in Berlin; talking over what options he had to get in the military, and what college incentives the Army offered after he was done.

Finding it too good to be true, Hamish grabbed his birth certificate and social security card, which his father kept in a locked truck in his bedroom on their family's homestead, and within a month, the recruiter snuck him to the testing center to take the ASVAB. He scored a 110, which meant the Army was opened to him. He chose generator mechanic, having some familiarity with machinery thanks to the auto classes he took in high school. After managing to pass the physical portion, he was good to go to basic in Fort Seal.

He told his family what he was going to do and why, and his father, enraged at his son's duplicity, threw him out of the house, yelling he would only be allowed back in when he stopped this nonsense. That same recruiter came and picked him up. He stayed at a homeless shelter for three days and went to basic after.

Since then, the only one of his family who talked to him at all was his little sister, Barbara. She sent him a letter thanks to a non-Amish friend he had in his hometown and to give her his letters in return.

Jenny learned this when she and a few of her girlfriends came back to the barracks one evening after a party and stumble upstairs and collapsed on the second floor, her head spinning from too many drinks. Hamish, who was returning a mop to the janitor's closet at that time, saw her and helped her get to her room, where Russel was already in. Russel helped Jenny back to her room, and Hamish returned to his.

The next morning, remembering Hamish's kindness, she went to go say thank you. She knocked on his door, and his roommate, Hickman as it so happens, let her in. She knocked on Hamish's door, who opened it, and before Jenny could say her rehearsed thank you, she noticed just how bare Hamish's room was. No TV, no game system, nothing. Only a quilt was on his bed and a few books on his desk, and his clothing. A Bible sat on the center of his desk, written in Pennsylvania Dutch.

She asked him about it, and he told her his story. Since then, they were friends, and later Hickman learning this, they became close amigos.

Now, she waited for him to speak.

"Aaron has cancer," he said finally, "in his brain."

"Oh, no," said Jenny, putting a hand on Hamish's shoulder. "Jacob, I'm sorry."

It was one of the few times she used Hamish's first name. Last names became more normal than first in the military. It was the last name that was on their tags, and thus that was how they were referred.

"She's asking me to come home and help."

"You going to talk to SGT Garcia?"

He shook his head; "About the situation, yes, but as for going home, we are too close to the field mission to put in a leave form.

Plus, Ohio is a red state, they won't let me go there unless it's an emergency leave."

"Well, tell her to call the Red Cross."

"She won't know how."

"Well, what about your father?"

"He still shuns me. He won't even take my call, and mother won't disobey him."

She kept her hand on his shoulder, and he sighed. "There are more Amish today than any point in history but we are a dying people, Dang. Genetic disorders are becoming more and more common. We are in a bottleneck. We keep going like this, the Amish will be unable to continue as they used to."

Jenny bit her lip, her heart going out to Hamish. They sat there, in silence for moment, until the door to the motorpool opened and Hickman stuck his head out.

"Yo," he hissed, "Sergeant is looking for you and..."

"Don't you dare warn them I'm coming, Specialist," snapped SGT Garcia, who blew passed Hickman, who now stood outside, awkwardly, Garcia glaring daggers at Jenny and Hamish.

"Why aren't you two inside? Lt. Perry and SFC Alibudbun are on their way and First Squad is always the first ready. So, why are you two not ready?"

Hamish, in answer, handed her his letter. She took it, and scanned it, then looked up with a look of concern and sorrow on her face.

"Oh, Hamish, I'm sorry."

"It's ok, Sergeant."

SGT Garcia, like Jenny and Hickman, were one of the few who knew Hamish's story. She felt for him, unable to imagine being separated from his family like that, not being allowed to help his brother.

"Your family call the Red Cross?"

Hamish shook his head and said, "My dad wouldn't do it anyways. He still refuses to talk to me."

"Your pops need to learn to let things go," she snapped, "Ain't right for a soldier being unable to comfort his brother."

Hamish nodded. Jenny and Hickman shocked at Garcia's bluntness.

"Ok," she said, "soon as we are done with the field, we are going to fill you out a leave form. Don't care if Fort Drum has put Ohio in the Red, we are doing it. Fuck coronavirus."

"Yes, Sergeant."

She nodded, then said, "Ok, back to work. We'll do our jobs and reminisce. Let's move people, we got a weekend to get ready for."

They responded and headed inside. Time for work.

CHAPTER TWO

The Clan

> "Full circle. A new terror born in death, a new superstition entering the unassailable fortress of forever. I am legend."
> — Richard Matheson, *I Am Legend*

Work for the soldiers for that day was average. The poker game didn't start until nine, but the sun was gone long before that and with it came the chilly night. Ragger, a nickname he took after he lost everything in the crash of 2008, shivered as his old Army jacket was doing little to protect him. He walked the street of Watertown, New York, where the homeless population was small and the winters were harsh and unforgiving. Ragger was one of the homeless.

He walked; pushing his few possessions in a shopping cart slowly down the street. The city was quiet. Since the outbreak of COVID, nights were not as lively as they used to be. Only a handful left their homes for the few vices available in Watertown. For Ragger though, these streets were home.

Watertown was a small town which once had a big city vibe. Home to over twenty thousand people, and a place of commerce. However, the city was starting to stagnate. The virus helped nothing. Occasionally, a few people pulled up to the bars, but that was it. Nothing much. Strip clubs, dance clubs, the virus, for the time being, took it all away. Fuck it, Ragger liked the quiet.

His long beard itched with lice, his coat had parasites, and he had a case of ringworm. But the quiet, god that was nice.

Ragger found his alley. The cops never bothered him there. He went into it, found his corner undisturbed, and made ready to sleep. That was until he felt the hand. It was like ice vice grip, which in an autumn night of upstate New York, was saying something. Something sharp dug into Ragger's shoulder. He was about to scream when he felt himself lifted up and forced to face his assailant. And what he saw made his bladder let go, one more smell to add to his growing collection.

The thing's skin was ivory white. It had pointed ears, no hair on its head, not even eyelashes. Its eyes were just pure black. No whites, no iris, just black pools. Its mouth, it was full of white teeth. No, more like fangs and sharp as a shark's. That's what caused Ragger to lose bladder control. Those teeth could rip him apart. Ragger saw the thing's free hand, which resembled more of a claw. It had five fingers, but where fingernails should have been, sharp, slashing claws replaced them. All five were thick, black, and sharp as daggers.

Ragger was about to scream when those teeth hit his neck, penetrating the artery, drinking the blood that flowed through Ragger's veins and draining the life from him. Slowly, he saw his whole life, his miserable life, flash, and when the thing finished, all that was left was a husk. For Ragger, this was the end of his life. For Orson Carter, this was just another meal. A disgusting meal, but a meal nonetheless. The man had more parasites in his blood than good blood. It was like comparing a Hungry Man frozen dinner to a five-star steak meal.

The fact was, Orson mused as he beheaded the corpse with his claws, it was becoming harder and harder to be a vampire anywhere in the world. The 1800's and 1900's were long gone.

With the advent of the internet, CCTV, satellite imagery, and those fucking camera phones, it meant the days of easy meals were gone. Now, they lived in the shadows, forced to feed on the SPAM of humanity. Orson missed the taste of humans who were well fed. His only hope was to find one who had drunk some booze beforehand to cover the taste of that homeless blood. God that was awful.

He remembered when he was first turned, 1904, Boston, where food was easy. Nowhere near as much connectivity as there was now. The crop was easier to harvest back then. Now it wasn't. He remembered 2013, Rose Butterwood, he had taken her and fed on her fresh, bittersweet, pregnant blood. After that, the massive manhunt forced his clan to uproot where they were staying and head to New York. Too many people were too connected. No more invisible men. Just a hope for a stray human to be found and used that wouldn't be missed in the greater social structure that the humans called civilization.

He picked up the decapitated corpse with ease, and the head, and zipped through town; going too fast for a human eye to track with ease. He got to the Black River and threw the corpse in the water. It would explain the blood loss and the fast decay. He was tempted to drink from the river to get the taste of parasites out of his mouth, but pure water was toxic to a vampire. He used it to wash the blood from his mouth, not daring to swallow any.

When done, he zipped back into town. He stopped in a shadow in a small collection of poorly maintained homes, pulled up the hood of his hoodie, put on a pair of sunglasses, a mask over his fangs and started walking to a Fastrac gas station on the other side of the street. He had to get the horrible taste out of his mouth. Cigarettes were the key. His ivory skin would draw eyes, but that could be explained away with albinism. He just needed this taste out of his mouth.

He entered the store, and he saw two soldiers looking over the beer section. God, he wished that he could drink alcohol as he did when he was human. He got a nice buzz off that stuff back in the day. The counter was free, and he heard the two soldiers whispering. One was a black kid who looked all but nineteen, and a 24-year old Sergeant.

The clerk at the register was an eighteen-year-old Palestinian girl with dark hair; curvy, sexy as hell. Oh god, Israel, the Six Day War, that had been a feast. Palestinian blood was so tasty. No, not here; he couldn't risk it. Too many cameras and people.

"Can I help you?" asked the girl, who covered her shock of the ivory skinned man with a smile under her mask.

"A pack of Pall Mall, menthol, please."

The girl nodded. Then Orson heard the whispered conversation of the two soldiers. His hearing was stronger than that of a human and their hushed conversation was audible to him as if they were standing behind him in line.

"Two weeks, next Wednesday," moaned the black soldier, "Middle of fucking nowhere and doing nothing but bullshit."

"Keep your voice down," said the Sergeant, "it won't be that bad."

"Fuck that, Sergeant," he whispered. "Shit, well, at least we can..."

"Sir," said the cashier, getting his attention.

"Sorry," said Orson, handing her a twenty. Taking the change, he left the store, unwrapped the cellophane from the cigs, and lit one. The smoke filled his long non-functioning lungs, and he let it out. It got rid of the dead taste in seconds. When he was back in the shadow, he zipped off, the conversation he overheard still in his mind.

When he started to reach the Black River, he saw other clan members coming in, after a night of disappointing feeding. Those vampires of Caucasian and Oriental descent skin turned ivory. Those of African, Arab, Latino, and Black Caribbean decent turned obsidian. Orson felt sorry for those vampires. They couldn't blend in as much as ivory vampires. But Orson didn't miss the looks of misery on their ivory and obsidian faces. For almost forty years, they had that look on their faces, feedings becoming harder and harder to perform; at least on this side of the world. Africa, the Middle East, Central Asia, those places still were easy picking, but too many clans were over there, and even in those countries, the risk of being discovered was greater in this period of time than any other.

More than twenty vampires soon reached the cave that lead to their current layer in Jefferson County. It was a cave on the bank of the river, hidden behind rocks, and the vampires entered it. The stone-walls, they were low, and Orson and the other vampires were forced to duck as they ran back to the nest.

The main chamber was filled with thirty-eight of the forty-one vampires the 12th Clan. The twelfth Elder, supposedly the greatest of this nest of ticks, was among them. That's what Orson thought of their nest, a nest of ticks. They sucked the blood of the weakest of the humans. Before this century, before the year 2000, they were kings of men. Now they were forced to hide, like rats, in the walls.

The nobility of being a vampire had long passed. Now, like the humans of the 1930's, they just scrapped by. Orson hated this, hated what the clan had become. Once, one was able to feed with the wars and tragedies from humanity. The Greco-Persian wars, the 100-year war, the American Revolution, the war of 1812, the Napoleonic Wars, the Bores War, WW I and II, Korea, Vietnam, Gulf War One, those were the glory years. Now, too much internet, not enough free food.

As he settled, finding his corner, he thought of the conversation he had overhead. Soldiers, isolated, god what a tasty treat, as he saw the midnight hunters turning to the opening of the nest and getting ready to feed. Isolated, fresh blood. Not the polluted blood of the homeless. It would be a feast, pure blood, only lightly seasoned with alcohol or tobacco one hoped.

He stood, making up his mind that he would go talk to the Elder. He started forward when Lee-Arne grabbed his arm. Lee-Arne was one of the obsidian vampires. She came from Australia, during the Japanese bombardment. The Elder turned her; her approval was worthy of the Elder's gift after she killed twenty Japanese soldiers in her desperation to resist the powerful force that threatened her home. She stood when nobody else would. She became a predator, the Japanese were her prey, and the Elder turned her to become a more effective killer. But again, those days were gone.

He stared at Lee-Arne. If he were human, her unearthly beauty would have given him an erection and drove him mad with lust. As an undead, his cock was a useless as a dead snake. He no longer had the sex drive he had in the 1900's. That was gone, replaced by the thirst. That need for blood; the pure blood. The clean taste, it was the closest that his kind got to an orgasm. Instead, the unclean blood of the homeless gave him an upset stomach at best.

Looking at him, she asked, "Why do you go seek the Elder?"

The semi-telepathy shared by the clan of vampires was an

incredible thing to witness. Human, at most, use only ten percent of communication via vocal transmission. Vampires, less than four percent of voice was used. Body language, ways of breathing, blinks, and gestures, they communicated a lot to a vampire. However, Orson thought it was best to use voice to get his message across.

"Feeding ground."

Lee-Arne's eyes opened wide, and her fanged mouth opened, a look that a cocaine fiend or an alcoholic would recognize. The last feeding ground they had was in Belarus, thank god for dumb asses in power. That had been fun but that had been almost forty years ago. Dear Lord, they needed a mass feeding.

Lee-Arne let him go. He walked down the tunnel. He passed other vampires, preparing to sleep, their coffins opened. That was another thing that bothered Orson. Before this century, the night belonged to the vampires. Now, they could barely have any fun outside except for feeding. A few hours were all they could risk. Before, Orson could sneak around human nightlife and enjoy the great music and plays of humanity. He hadn't seen a stage play in almost 30 years.

Before reaching the Elder's chamber, he passed what looked like a dried mummy of a Buddhist monk in meditation. Under its ivory fresh, Orson saw bones of the ribs showing. Its legs were crossed and seemed unnaturally thin and long. It was Legwang, the monk, and the second oldest vampire in the clan. At 12,000 years old, the second oldest after the Elder, he witnessed the rise and fall of thousands of civilizations all around the world, following the Elder as he went, they were feeding on the freshest crop humanity had to offer. Now, instead of being the prince and the right-hand man of the Elder, Legwang spent his days as a scholar and in meditation. They had been in Watertown for almost a week. Legwang had been in this mummified state for almost 40 years, the Clan dragging his carcass across the world as they went. Useless. He passed the corpse and went into the private cave of the Elder.

The Elder was over seven feet tall and like Orson and a few others of the Clan, he was completely bald, with the exception of a long, sweeping mustache. However, he had a pronounced brow, and a sloped forehead. At being over 15,000 years old, some say he was older than humanity itself, his face looking slightly Neanderthal-like. His wide, flat nose, and large teeth feed into this rumor well. The Elder, his eyes narrowed, his fanged mouth exposed, and arms crossed across a chest almost as wide as two men. He was dressed in a black robe, making him look almost like a monk in a Christian monastery.

Orson instantly went to one knee in a suggestion of fidelity, eyes closed, head lowered. The Elder's shadow came over to him, as if he knew what was to be said in the cave. Orson again was forced to wonder if the dried-up mummy of Legwang was somehow able to communicate with the Elder, that husk having a deeper communication with this ancient being. It was possible. There were only twelve Elders in the whole world, and Orson had never met another, so who knew what they were fully capable of doing.

"Speak," said the Elder, his voice like thunder.

Orson looked up at his maker; the creature over him appeared god like in this lightless void. And in a way, he was a god, the vampire that turned Orson in 1904, finding him worthy of Immortality, giving new life and purpose to him. Creating a new being from the creature, Orson had once been, saving him from the human world where he didn't fully belong.

"I have knowledge of a feeding field."

That peaked the Elder's interest.

"What is this field you speak of."

"I overheard some soldiers from the local base. They are going on a field mission."

For almost a whole minute, the Elder stood in silence, then a great booming laughter filled the cave, and it shook Orson to his soul. When the Elder was done, he shook his head and spoke, speaking with a dreadful and sarcastic tone.

"So, your plan is to go to a military training field, and what, feed upon them and hope the Army won't take notice?"

"Master, we can take steps to cut them off. We have the ability."

"You fool," he said, "they would hunt us down. Soldiers are not like other humans. When one attacks them, they won't give up that easily. They are crafty, resourceful, and their brotherhood will bring them to obliterate us. They are almost as dangerous as the old hunters."

Orson, on regular nights, would never question the word of the Elder, but the taste of that wretch's blood still polluted his mouth, and he was desperate for good blood. This need emboldened him to speak.

"Master, every night, it gets harder and harder to hunt. Once, we moved and fed, always in the wake of human misery. Now we slink, feared of being caught on camera, making us coward in these caves with our coffins. Forced to feed on the lowest of our prey. To survive, we might have to take bolder steps."

The Elder was silent for a long moment, and Orson hoped he got through to him. That was, until, a large hand wrapped around his neck, and brought him hanging, face to face with the Elder.

While oxygen had not been needed for Orson's survival over these past hundred plus years, separation of the head from the body was just as fatal for his kind as it was for humans. He feared this to be his fate as the elder brought his face forward to his, their noses almost touching.

"You speak as a hunter. That I can understand. You see yourself as a hunter. You're stronger, faster, more attune to the world than any human. You can see, hear, and smell better than them. But let me put your mind in its place. You are a parasite, as I am. You leach off their race. Without them and their blood to sustain us, we would be weak. But they don't need us. One human may not seem like a threat to you, but when you draw their attention, one human becomes two, two becomes a dozen, and more and more will come, and we will fall under their weight. There are only a few dozen of us at any time among the twelve clans. Too many of us at any one time will draw their attention. We learned a hard lesson after what happened to the 13th Clan."

The 13th clan; Orson knew the story well. The clan had traveled to India, following the trail of Alexander the Great's Army, feeding on the edges of the battles at night. It wasn't until when they reached India that they attacked a village. The clan was only ten strong, but against a village of only a few hundred, it should have been an easy feed. However, as the clan attacked the village, an old man came out of the main hut that was used as a sort of town center back then. He was more than a hundred some said. Old and wrinkled, his blood was long past his prime, but he came out and challenged the Elder of the Thirteenth. The elder laughed and zipped forward. He grabbed this old thing by the throat, opened his jaws, and bit the man on the neck; tasting his poor excuse for blood.

What that Elder didn't know was that the old man had a

sword hidden behind his back. The Indian man with strength, even as the blood drained from his body, swung and hit the vampire in the back of the neck and beheaded the Elder. He also cut his own throat in the process.

That had been a first in history. Many humans had killed average vampires throughout the centuries, but until that time, not one had ever killed an Elder. The vampires of the Thirteenth Clan were left homeless, directionless, and ending up without a clan. Most would die, but one or two were welcomed into other clans, but that was the end of the Thirteenth.

Orson knew this, yet, all that fresh blood. He stopped talking, and the Elder dropped him to the ground and snarled, "Speak no more of this foolishness."

Orson was thrown from the chamber, nearly hitting the mummified Legwang. He lay there, angry and embarrassed for a moment. Then got up and started to go to his coffin. He was stopped by Lee-Arne. Her obsidian skin blended so well in the dark cave, he nearly missed her.

"Will we feast?"

At first, Orson was about to say no, but then a thought came to him. He looked at Lee-Arne, who could tell what he was thinking, and she nodded, not wanting the Elder to hear. Much work had to be done, but as of now, it was time to rest. The next night was when his work began.

CHAPTER THREE

Weekend

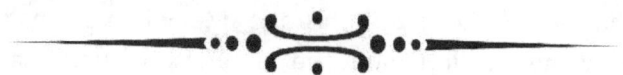

"Even when we're apart, we'll be looking at the same sky!"

— L.J. Smith, *Daughters of Darkness*

Friday night, around six, Jenny arrived at Madam Roseta's home in Even Mills, a small town outside of Watertown and Fort Hood. Even Mills was connected to LeRay, but it was its own town. In that town, there was a small, unassuming house outside the main square. But in that house was one of Jenny's greatest teachers. She got out of her car and headed inside. Getting to the front door of the white panel house, she knocked, and the door was answered in seconds.

If one looked at Madam Roseta, one would assume that she was a woman in her early thirties. In reality, she was forty-eight. However, years of dancing, healthy living, and despite one not willing to fully accept this, wine drinking helped her retain her youth. She had large, dark eyes, black raven hair, a thin nose, smooth, flawless skin, natural red lips, a thin, very shapely body, small but high breasts, long legs that had hit many stages from Romania to America. Once, she had been world famous. Now, she passed her skills to the next generation.

"Hey," said Jenny with a smile, but it vanished when Roseta snapped.

"Let me see your hands."

Jenny held them out for Roseta's inspection; felling like she was back in basic, her stomach churning, hoping her uniform was just right.

"No oil, good," Roseta said.

Relief hit her hard and she smiled.

Roseta said, "Go to the bathroom. Change. We have much work to do."

Jenny went into the home. It was well maintained and charming. The living room had been converted into a dance studio, the ceiling raised to allow the students to dance unencumbered with a mirrored wall. A bar stretched across the front wall and covering what once had been a window. The rest of the house was normal looking. A whitewash kitchen was to the left of the studio, and a hall lead to the bathrooms, a master bedroom, and a second bedroom. Jenny changed in the bathroom. She removed her pink shirt, bra, and jeans, and put on a black leotard, stockings, and the ballet shoes her mother got her for her birthday last year. Jenny sighed. She wasn't sure how she felt about her parents lately. When she was a child, she was very close to them, but now she felt something of a break between them. She called when she could, but that was it. Still, it seemed they were coming around to her becoming a dancer, so that was something.

When she got out, Roseta inspected her like a drill instructor, making sure each of Jenny's clothing items were set for comfort and best for her flexibility. And Roseta conducted her through her stretches; stretches more intense than any Army PT session. Roseta inspected her and helped her make tiny adjustments.

Roseta's knowledge and skill came from her time at the

Romanian National Opera, in Bucharest, and when she worked for the Royal Winnipeg Ballet Company in Canada. She worked at both for a collective thirteen years. She was top billing in all her shows, a premiere dancer. That was until she had a daughter. She had fallen in love with an American Vet, who worked behind the stage for the Winnipeg Ballet shows. He was strong, kind, and most importantly, loved to dance. The tragedy: he couldn't. He lost his right leg in Afghanistan, only surviving thanks to an old friend in Montreal. A former Captain Holden of the Canadian Special forces who pulled him out of there. Roseta noticed him always looking at her during her shows. He never did it at any other time, just when she was on stage. When she asked him why, he explained that he had also considered dancing as a career, but losing his leg took that away. Now he could only watch the best. She felt something for him and started dating him, fell in love, married him, and ended up having his daughter.

Roseta didn't mean to stop dancing after she had her child, but that choice had been taken away from her. There was a complication, and the C-section prevented her from being able to dance how she once did. But she still had the skills. Her husband, who knew what it was like to lose something he loved, encouraged her to find other ways to do the thing she loved: ballet. She began to write ballets and teaching others how on the side. Four of her pieces had been produced and directed by her in New York and now she was Jenny's teacher.

Roseta was very hard on Jenny but that was because she saw how much Jenny loved it; she was amazing. In fact, Roseta was helping her make contacts by sending Jenny's portfolio and videos of her dancing to schools and to companies across North America, both the USA and Canada. So far, while there were no bites there were nibbles; wanting more examples of the dance.

After two and a half hours of practice, Roseta smiled and said, "You are doing well. I'd say you're almost at my level as an individual."

Jenny smiled at this, patting down her exposed flesh with her towel.

"But," said Roseta, "We still need to see how you perform with a partner."

Jenny bit her lip nervously.

"I've never danced with a partner," she said, "wouldn't that take away from my own performance?"

Roseta shook her head.

"No. While dancing with a partner, a man may lead, but the woman is always the center of attention. When she is on stage, she draws all eyes. I know; I was that center."

"Still..."

Roseta put her hands on Jenny's shoulders and said, "Learning how to trust a partner now will put you way ahead of the game. You have a gift, Jenny, and you only have six months before you go home. Trust me."

"Okay."

She packed her stuff. Before she left, she was given a sudden urge to ask a question about her mentor.

"Roseta, what was your favorite ballet before you stopped dancing?"

Madam Roseta paused and put away some props that Jenny used in her practice. She turned, her lovely face having a small and distant smile on her lips.

"That would be the last one I did before I got pregnant."

"What was that?"

Roseta smiled and said, slowly, "Dracula."

Jenny was surprised. She had heard of the character, and

seen her share of Dracula movies, but she never knew there was a Dracula ballet.

"Dracula?"

"Yes." Roseta chuckled, "You didn't know there was a ballet like that?"

Roseta shook her head, surprised of the fact there was a ballet based on such an iconic character.

"Well it was years ago, and I played the character of Lucy. It was one of my favorites. It was telling that same story in a way that wasn't done before."

"I've only seen a few Dracula movies."

"Have you read the book?" asked Roseta.

"No."

Roseta smiled and said "You want to have a cup of coffee. It will come with a great story."

Jenny curiously consented and joined Roseta for two hot mugs of instant coffee. Adding cream and sugar, the two sat across the small table. After a sip, Roseta began her story.

"As you know I grew up in Romania. Brasov, to be precise. There was Bran Castle. Some say Dracula lived up there though it isn't true. There was a historical figure called Dracula, a prince by the name of Vlad the Impaler. I did read the novel written by Bram Stoker and enjoyed it. His Dracula had nothing to do with Romania, more precisely Transylvania when it was part of Hungary. But when I was a girl I heard other stories. Stories of vampires not like Dracula. They were different stories. The story of the vampire has been told around the world and all of them are different and have different names. Strigoi, Vampyr, Nosferatu, but as a little girl the stories terrified me. Even when I joined the ballet, the stories my father told me as a baby still haunted me.

"He was walking in the village he grew up in. It was a cold November night. The village was hunkering down for the winter. My father was with a friend. They were playing ball, running down the street and tossing it to each other via their feet. They were nearing the edge of the village. They weren't supposed to be that far but boys will be boys."

She shuttered then, this part of the story always caused her horror.

"They heard a scream. The scream of a woman. My father would say it sounded like a death call. But as two curious boys they went to investigate. They ran a quarter mile out of town. They ran; curiosity making them hurry. Then they came to a grassy patch outside of the village.

"They saw an old woman dressed in a long thick winter dress laying on the ground, her body convulsing as if in pleasure. But the action they saw wasn't any act of pleasure. She was set upon by a creature. The boys stared in horror and their screams caused it to let go of the woman's neck. It had skin the color of midnight, black eyes, a mouth full of sharp fang like teeth, and hands that were claws. Its lips and chin covered in blood from the woman's torn throat; blood covering her face."

She shuttered again.

"My father told me of the smell that hit him like that of decay. He didn't know if it came from the woman or the creature, the Strigoi, as he called it. Both the boys screamed and the creature screamed; its voice almost unearthly.

"They ran back to the village. They were screaming the whole way. They swore they heard the creature behind them but when they turned their heads there was nothing. Nobody believed their tale."

Jenny saw the horror in her face, the real horror of one

actually scared of the story she was telling. Then she looked up and smiled.

"I feared that tale for most of my life until I danced Dracula. When I was asked to do it, I was scared. The thought of them hiring an actual Strigoi made me fearful. But it was a leading role and I decided to accept it."

Roseta then had a dreamy quality on her face.

"But then I started dancing the part of Lucy. I was hooked even when Dracula came on the stage. It got me over my fears. Dancing got rid of the boogie man and let me see how one can see something differently: just add it to something I love."

Jenny finished her coffee and asked one more question.

"So you got a partner in mind to get me over my fear when I am back?"

Roseta smiled, "You get over you're concern about that. I promise to find you the best I can."

The two smiled, stood, embraced, and went their separate ways. Jenny got back to her barracks at Fort Drum about twenty minutes later. She got back, locked her door, and headed into the building nodding at the CQ personnel and headed upstairs. She got back to her room, nodded at her roommate whose door was open. She entered her room and stripped off her leotard. She felt the cool feeling of air on her sweaty skin. Enjoying it for a long moment; her nipples hardened. She then showered and changed into a tee shirt and pajama pants and was about to leave when she unplugged her phone and noticed a note on the screen. "Missed Call: Mom."

Jenny sighed. She hadn't decided to call her mom and dad. They were not thrilled that she decided to join the Army for the college money. She wanted to dance so badly and would do anything to make that dream come true. Though her parents came to the states after the Vietnam War, as children they were always resentful of the fact they were living in a country that left them exiled from their homeland. Even worse, their daughter was more westernized than they liked. With her style, love of movies and ballet obsession, they thought maybe they should send her to the homeland to get some roots. Instead, she fled to the Army. Like Hamish, Jenny's parents didn't come to her basic graduation. However, unlike Hamish, her parents still talked to her at least once in a while. She knew they loved her but she wanted to live her own life; not bound to the two countries that had a hold of her life. She shook her head. She'd call her later. Right now; poker night.

She went to the third floor; the blue walls reminding her of a lake she visited as a child. She got to room 312, Hickman and Hamish's room, knocked and it opened.

"How were the dance lessons?" asked Garcia, her lips having a sly smile.

"It went well" said Jenny smiling back but a little surprised "Sorry, I thought..."

"I invited Jackson and Sosa, but they were busy so it's just you, me, Hamish, and Hickman."

Jenny smiled, nodded, and entered. Garcia only came to poker night when she felt she was needed. She liked the game but as an NCO she couldn't fraternize. So to get past that, she invited all her soldiers and NCOs to a game; when she was needed. Sosa, who had her wife, never came. Jackson was passed out on Jack Daniels at the moment. Her NCOs were never interested. So she got the three soldier that needed there NCO the most. Plus, a twenty dollar buy in they all looked forward to winning.

Jenny went to her pajama pants pocket and pulled out her

twenty-dollar bill and threw it into the winner's box as soon as she entered Hamish's room. A small card table was set up. The top was green felt. Hamish sat on one side, his serene face, shuffling cards. While most of his people would frown on Hamish's card slinging, Hamish hadn't technically joined the Amish church yet so he was under no obligation to obey their rules. Hickman sat next to him, on the side of the table facing the closet. He wore sunglasses, had a Boston Lager on the table, fingering the pile of chips; he looked like a young Wesley Snipes.

Garcia and Jenny joined. Jenny sat across from Hickman; Garcia across from Hamish. Their chips were already on the table. Jenny was handed a bottle of Vodka and some orange juice along with a glass. Quickly making her drink, she was ready. So was Sergeant Garcia who had a Manhattan, the way her dad made it as she said; and Hamish's hard cider. Hamish didn't drink anywhere as much as the others, but he did for poker night. He was a fiend at the game ever since Hickman showed him how to play. Like a crack casino dealer, he dealt the cards out for Texas Hold'em. Jenny got two aces to start. Everyone else kept their faces as still as possible. Hickman, being the big ante, threw down a white chip worth a dollar. Garcia, being the little ante, threw in fifty cents; not looking up from her cards. She had nothing.

Half an hour into the game Hickman's and Garcia's piles were half their original size. Jenny's pile was decent but Hamish's pile was larger than all of theirs put together.

"Shit, man," said Hickman as Hamish sorted his new chips. "How the hell do you keep winning?"

Hamish cracked a small smile; the first in a half hour.

"Just get lucky."

"That ain't luck," snapped Hickman, "that's some voodoo shit."

Hamish's smile seemed to lessen somewhat. He and the others noticed a tone in Hickman's voice.

"You seem, my friend, a little strained. Is something the matter?"

Hickman took off his sunglasses and rubbed his eyes as if tired. He took a deep breath and said, "My dad got a call from my mom. She wants to talk to me."

They all stared. Tone Hickman was born in an apartment in the slums of Detroit to two loving parents. Patrick Hickman and Ayesha Hickman were two young African American teenagers, kicked out of their homes, after it was discovered that Ayesha was pregnant. Forced on the streets, the two found a shelter and Tone Hickman was born there. Later in life, he would go by his last name more than his first. At first life was fine. Though living in one of the worst parts of Detroit, the Hickman's managed to carve out a bit of a life. Patrick found work with a construction company and Ayesha raised the child and sewed neighbors clothing.

Things changed though when Tone Hickman turned two. Ayesha started to become more and more restless; sleeping and eating less and reading the Bible more. Patrick was concerned but scared to seek help. Black people who got into any government system rarely could go free of it, as Tone Hickman put it. As long as Tone Hickman was safe and well taken care of, that was all that mattered.

October 1999, Patrick came home after a long day at a building site and heard soft sobbing. Walking in, Patrick found the sounds were coming from Tone Hickman's room. He walked down the short hall and entered; opening the door as softly as possible. What he saw sent his mind reeling. Ayesha, a loving carrying young mother of twenty, was choking her son. The two-year-old was clawing his small hands at his mother while turning a deathly black. Ayesha was praying as she did this.

"God, forgive me. Though I know he is my son, I know he is destined for darkness and I cannot..."

Patrick sprang into action. Patrick was not a violent man by nature. At this point he had never even raised his voice to his wife or son; he grabbed his wife from behind, pulling her, kicking and screaming, off his son. The boy took a gasp and Patrick held his arm around his wife's neck, waiting ten seconds, until she went limp and he let her drop to the floor. He then ran to Hickman who was crying, scooped him up and ran them both out of the apartment down the hall to a neighbor. It was a couple of Nigerian illegal immigrants, a man and a woman, and after barging in explained what just happened. Luckily, the Nigerians understood English and they agreed to watch over Hickman and let Patrick call 911 before going back to his apartment. He sat by the front door listening to his wife sobbing.

The cops came and after arresting Ayesha and getting a statement out of Patrick they left; leaving Patrick and the scared, but calmed down, Hickman behind. Ayesha was institutionalized and Patrick, after desperately searching for a company that needed an experienced builder, relocated himself and Tone to Queens. Tone had not seen his mother since.

Hamish and Jenny learned this after Hickman got extremely drunk one night and after spilling his guts of Fireball then spilling his guts of his woes. He had never met his mother before his memories were formed, but the guilt he felt, the guilt his father never put upon him, but he felt after learning what happened, haunted him. It made him feel like he was the cause of his mother's insanity.

Garcia also knew everything, put an arm on Hickman and

said, "What do you think you should do?"

Hickman shrugged, "I don't know."

Hamish smiled slightly and said, "I know your pain for it is what I feel when I think of my brother."

Hickman, knowing Hamish's story as well, embraced his friend. "Thanks, man."

Garcia smiled at that as did Jenny. Garcia then spoke.

"We enjoy what is left of the weekend then we focus on how to help you. There is nothing that can be done at the moment and we have a field coming up. We will have more time to make decisions on what is to be done. Until then; two bucks."

They all felt better and Hickman, as a final remark, said, "Well, this can't get any worse."

In a few days he would regret those words. Until then, the night ended. Hamish wining eighty dollars and the rest going home packing.

Jenny went back to her room. The six screw drivers she drank messed with her mind. Lying in bed, and after having two pisses, she felt a need: a want. The last time she had sex was a year ago, from a soldier long since gone. Not wanting to hunt, she pulled out her phone, looked up Literotica and found a Zeus story of when he took Europa. She had herself a little fun playing with herself, reading, until she ended up gasping. The world melted away. Seemingly, without darkness, only the intense pleasure she gave herself mattered. Once done, she went to the bathroom; washed her hands and fell asleep. At the moment, the state of bliss is keeping her hopeful.

CHAPTER FOUR

General Bryant's Uninvited House Guest

"If somebody wants to be your enemy there's only one thing you can do. You give them exactly what they want. It confuses them and makes them wonder what you're up to."
— David Wellington *13 Bullets*

Friday turned into Saturday morning then Saturday night. For Jenny, most of the soldiers of Fort Drum, the civilians of Watertown and the surrounding towns and villages, it was just a normal day off. For those who had it as normal as you could get, with the pandemic. For others, just a normal workday, the only thing of note was that one of the local bums, who went by the name Ragger, seemed not around as of late. Not that they cared, just a thing to note.

But when night came, it would come with a fully formed plan in Orson's mind. A plan not enacted since that feeding in Belarus.

Orson awoke, his mouth full of dirt. It was always this way. Being of the undead, Orson usually slept in a coffin during the day. This wasn't because of tradition, though that was part of it. It was because a coffin could hold the dirt, that unholy dirt, to which they were buried in after they were bitten and sucked dry by the Elder. Who then gave his new children a drop of his own blood and thus they were reborn. Reborn into what was once an exciting life of flowing human suffering, to get the best meals, now one of desperate feeding on whatever scraps of people they could find isolated and alone.

Orson opened his coffin and rose from his dirt. The dirt acted as both a protection from that sun and the only place he could rest. Vampires cannot rest unless they rest in the earth they were buried but there were ways around it. When needed to go long distances away from the nest, one only needed to carry a small amount of the unholy dirt. When they needed to rest and their coffin wasn't available, they'd use their small amount of dirt, put it on the ground, mixed it with the rest of it and then a vampire can rest in that dirt, no problem. When awake, just take some of that earth with them as well for the next morning. Coffins were used because they could hold a lot of dirt and well, they were oddly comfortable.

Rising from the dirt, Orson felt it fall away from his body. Before baby wipes, vamps would always have a little of that dirt cling to them making their flesh more of a telltale sign that they were a vampire. Unable to go into water, the baby wipe proved to be a lifesaver. Changing out of his clothing, he grabbed one of the wipes, wiped off his ivory flesh, then put on his new clothing. When done, Lee-Arne joined him. Her obsidian flesh cleaned of dirt as well. They both wore hoodies, jeans, and running shoes. They also had their sunglasses to cover their eyes and masks to cover their fangs. The coronavirus; what fun. Vampires don't fear things like viruses and bacteria, as it does their prey, but the mask let them move more freely in the human world.

They headed out, zipping out with twenty other hungry vampires. Then, went outside the cave, they broke ranks. Vampires never hunted in packs. It was rare nowadays for two vampires to hunt together, but not unheard of. The others watch

Orson and Lee-Arne go, with only passing interest. There was a homeless camp they were heading to, deep in the woods, and they intended to reach it. Let those two hunt their own prey.

Lee-Arne and Orson zipped down the road until they reached the town of Black River. They zipped through, barely paying attention to it until they reached a place called Black River Gate. The gate to the base was blocked by a big slab of concrete and barbed wire fence. For a human it'd be dangerous to try and climb. For these two, however, a simple hop twenty feet into the air was all that was needed.

They landed catlike on the ground and zipped through, Orson was listening for the man he had heard in the store. For three hours, they ran through the sleeping base, only hiding when they saw a car coming. They found barracks but Orson didn't hear the man. Hoping to god he didn't live off the base, Orson kept moving with Lee-Arne going from barracks to barracks until they came to one of the last barracks they found on the post. Then he heard it. The sounds of over two hundred soldiers snoring, breathing, talking; he was able to pick out one voice, the black kid from the store. He smiled and looked at the sign: 514 and 517 Company Barracks 549 Support Battalion. This was it. Orson was about to enter when Lee-Arne put a clawed hand on his shoulder stopping him.

"No," she whispered, "we'll be spotted too quickly."

"We need information if we are going to do this!" snapped Orson. "What do you suggest?"

"Come with me," she whispered.

They dashed up the road, their speed hard to track with a human eye, until they came to a pair of buildings about a quarter mile up, in under thirty seconds. They came to the first: a long building that was dark but had several signs on it. One was 514

MSC Company. Then she pointed to the other building at a ninety-degree angle from the first. It had a metal roof and red brick frame; the front door on the far front right side. She smiled and Orson saw why. The sign read 549 Support Battalion. They heard breathing inside; the breathing of only one human. They walked slowly, keeping their excitement down with effort. They entered the first and then the second pair of doors. Inside was a narrow hall with grayish carpet, a white ceiling, and blue walls.

They smiled and saw a square hole in the wall next to an open door revealing a room within. Within it was a desk, two chairs, one being occupied by a tough looking white guy with a buzz cut and brown eyes. He wore a green and brownish uniform. On his chest were three Velcro strips the first showed the saying 'US Army'. They second showed his name, Rodrigues. The third was a rank that of Staff Sergeant. One shoulder displayed the USA flag on a Velcro patch. The other was a patch that said 'Mountain'. Below it a square, with black edges, a greenish-gray field and two cross swords the symbol of the 10th Mountain Division. Not that the vampires knew or cared they just wanted information that this NCO could provide.

However, it took Orson a minute to compose himself for he smelled the man's blood. Its aroma was enticing to Orson. It wasn't opened aired or infected with lice and blood worms. Instead, it was strong, healthy and a scent of menthol came from it along with the smell of stale smoke, making this man's blood so appealing to Orson. But he held back his want. This one snack wasn't worth wasting when he could possibly provide a feast.

The tired looking NCO looked up, yawning and saw the two figures in hoodies, masks, and sunglasses. He stood about to chew them out, assuming they were soldiers, when he noticed what they looked like under their hoodies: one as pale as bone the other black as night.

"What the..." started the NCO when Orson took off his sunglasses revealing black eyes. At first this man named Rodrigues almost reeled in fear. But then the eyes changed. What Rodrigues saw he couldn't explain but they mesmerized him. They drew him, holding him still, and he was soon in a trancelike state; similar to that of being hypnotized. It was a skill few vampires possessed and Orson wasn't anywhere near as good as the Elder but he knew enough to control this one with no issues.

"Do you hear me human?" asked Orson.

"Yeah." he murmured, "They're so beautiful. What are in those eyes?"

"I'll tell you but first you need to answer my question."

The man's face was slack now and a little drool was coming out the corner of his mouth.

"Okay," he said faintly, his voice thick as one who was sleep talking with a fake Southern accent. "It's so beautiful."

"Where is the 514 going on Wednesday?" asked Orson ignoring the urge to bit and drink this human.

"Field exercise," muttered the man, "it is a battalion event for the 549. They're going to Site Indigo about three hours northeast of here. Middle of nowhere; closest town over seventy miles away."

"How many people will be there?" asked Orson.

"Other than rear guard, about 849 people give or take. My god what's in those eyes?"

More drool came from Rodrigues's mouth dripping on to his uniform in a steady string. This interested Orson little though, he did find the look of the drooling man somewhat funny. The number did interest him. Eight hundred and forty-nine healthy men and women. Oh god; it made his mouth water. If he were still human, he might have an erection.

"What are they bringing?" asked Orson.

"In general?"

"Yes."

"Usual: tents, trucks, rifles. They're bringing some ammo but not much. Just some for target practice with their Carbines. They are going to be sending some extra later on, a truck later when the rest arrive or the next day."

Orson nodded. Bullets did hurt but it took a lot of them to kill a vampire, a few hundred at least. Their speed made it difficult for them to be hit and their rapid healing made it even more difficult to take down. Not a big problem for the undead.

"How long will they be cut off?"

"They won't be," murmured Rodrigues, "they'll have radios, cellphone, too."

Orson hissed. Radios he could easily destroy but 849 cellphones, that's a problem.

"Who can prevent them from bringing them?"

"The commander, Lt. Colonel Swarts could but his people would protest. Soldiers don't like being cut off from their loved ones. He wouldn't give that kind of order."

"Who commands him?"

"The brigade commander Colonel Norris but again, she wouldn't do it either."

"Above her?"

"Division Brigade General Bryant. Nobody would countermand that order; it's coming all the way from the top."

"Where can I find him?"

"He lives on the other side of the post; his home is among the largest and fanciest here on Fort Drum. You can't miss it."

"Will he be alone?"

"He has a wife."

Orson nodded.

"Now, tell me what's in those eyes?"

"What do you see?" asked Orson.

Rodrigues' mouth formed into a smile, that of a man having a dirty thought.

"I see myself railing Selena Gomez, Jennifer Lopez, Shakira, and so many others."

Orson smiled and decided to reward him for his great assistance.

"Here is what I'm going to do. Do you have a wife?"

"Yes," he said, "she's beautiful but plain in some ways."

"Well, whenever you fuck her and you think about these other women, she will look like the one you're thinking of; from this day on."

"You promise?"

"Yes," Orson said with a smile. "Now, we are leaving and you won't remember anything you said or us. Understand?"

"Huh-uh."

"You will wake up after you hear the door shut."

"Okay."

The two vampires left leaving SSG Rodrigues dazed, but back to himself after they were gone; the memory of their encounter no longer in his mind.

General Bryant sat outside in a plaid sweater and jeans. He had a thousand things to do a day but this moment eleven o'clock, or 2300, hours was his. No military, no bullshit, no COVID no UCMJs, just peace. His wife was long asleep and he would join her in an hour. God, she made it possible to do his line of work, to make it through the day, supporting him as much as she did.

She was an amazing woman, one of a kind and he swore half the time she kept the division together on her own. Seven more months and it was over he had promised her and he was going to keep that promise of that long thought of and dreamt retirement package. Just her, their three children, and their four grandkids. They would move to Lowville, a town she loved, and would spend their remaining years finding things to do. Whether it'd be reading, gardening, or taking trips to visit there extended family. He was even thinking about small town politics but he wasn't sure about that quite yet. They would see if he could handle civilian life first. Maybe start with a hobby: wood carving, sailing, rafting. Or maybe just do what he was doing now, enjoying the quiet.

He enjoyed the night and noticed a deer scampering away across his lawn. He smiles, his eye's following it. Fort Drum, a lot of deployments happened up here but when you had time to just sit and smell the roses it was quite lovely. The woods, the animals, it was the best base he ever served at just for the scenery. Even with COVID, it was a sight.

He blinked and then fell back as when he opened his eyes he saw a person standing in front of him. It wore a hoodie and jeans but its hands were claws, its skin, ivory colored like bone. Its teeth, my goodness, they looked as sharp as shark teeth. Its ears were larger than a human's and pointed. Oh, God and Jesus; what was he looking at? Where was his gun?

Then he saw the eyes, those cold black eyes and saw something so beautiful. He saw him and his wife sitting on the porch of the house they bought in Lowville, just enjoying their coffee, peacefully, no fear of the virus or the wars or him going overseas again. His mind went slack, relaxed via the images he saw: that of all his dreams coming true.

"Do you like what you see?" asked the being.

"Yes."

"Then do as I command and it will all come true."

***

Colonel Norris, commanding officer of the 802 Command Brigade which included the 549 Support Battalion awoke with a start; her eyes flying to her cellphone. She moaned. Why now? She just got to sleep. Whoever this caller was and if it was a soldier acting stupid; that soldier was going to get busted down to private.

She picked it up and saw it was Brigade General Bryant. Christ, what did he want?

She answered.

"Colonel Norris speaking."

"Colonel," said the voice over the line, "sorry to wake you up."

"Yes, General that is okay."

"Colonel, I believe you have a field mission coming up with one of your battalions."

Norris shook her head and responded "Yes, sir. The 549 Support Battalion. They head out this Wednesday."

"Colonel, I have additional instructions you will add to their mission."

Okay, this was different. "I'm listening, sir."

"All who are participating in this field exercise, their cellphones are to be confiscated upon weapons draw and be left in the arms room for safe keeping."

All sense of tiredness left her. She had to have heard that wrong. It had to just be tiredness that was muddling her mind she missed hearing the General's words.

"Sir? I'm sorry I don't think I got…"

"You heard me."

This couldn't be real. Why would the soon to be retiring Division commander care about this at all? Hell, she always had a cellphone with her during field mission. She needed it for her job and it wasn't an option for her.

"Sir, why are we confiscating the soldier cellphones? And is this just enlisted or…"

"I'll answer the second question first: all soldiers; NCOs and officers including the Battalion Commander; the Battalion XO; and Battalion Commander Sergeant Major. As for the first, lately I've come to believe those soldiers are spending too much time on their phones and not enough on training which is the purpose of these missions. This is a test bed to see if there is marked improvement during this mission without a distraction of those infernal devices."

All Norris could think was: *had this man just lost his mind?* One thing she knew about soldiers, they like to be connected to their families for the most part. Plus, nowadays they used their phones for everything from making calls to paying bills. No phones meant they couldn't do important business, pay mortgages or bills and that wasn't right.

"Sir…"

"Are you questioning my orders?" snapped General Bryant.

I'm questioning your sanity, she thought, but surrendered and said, "No, sir."

"Good; make it happen, Colonel."

The General hung up. She sighed, staring at her phone. There was a knock on the door and a voice of a twelve-year-old girl saying, "Mommy, are you okay?"

"I'm fine," she said. "Go back to bed, sweetie."

Soft footsteps patted away from the master bedroom door. Norris sighed and called Lt. Colonial Swarts. Well, so much for a drama free weekend.

CHAPTER FIVE

Bad News on Monday, Silver and Garlic

"Judge us not equally Abraham. We may all deserve hell but some of us deserve it sooner than others"
— Seth Grahame-Smith *Abraham Lincoln Vampire Hunter*

The time for PT came again on Monday morning. As did PMCS, but that would come later. The weekend for soldiers meant drinking, partying, fucking, and sleep with no end in sight. Monday was the worst day for a soldier. It was the time when a soldier needed to be a soldier again and not a frat boy or girl they became on the weekend. The fun over, the bottles were stored or thrown away, moaning with hangovers, and with the jizz no longer shooting, they stood in formation; tired and grumpy.

Jenny, Hamish, and Hickman were no exception. Jenny had one too many screwdrivers over the weekend. Hamish, though he only had two hard ciders, also felt woes from worrying about his brother. Hickman smelled like a brewery; his very breath could get one drunk if they inhaled the scent. His eyes were almost pure red. Even Garcia looked haggard, but not nearly as much as the rest of her soldiers.

Jackson and Sosa were also there shaking their heads. Sengel and Pag also looked a little off, but they were following Garcia's example; they were not immune to the seduction of the weekend. Still, first Squad was there and that was all that mattered to Garcia.

"I swear to God," said Hickman, "if we run today, I'm going to die. Just drop dead."

"Not my fault you had sixty beers this weekend," whispered Garcia harshly, "Christ, how did you manage it without dying?"

"Too much experience."

"Swear to God, Hickman, I'm making you go to an AA meeting when we get back from the field."

"Don't think you can make that an order, Sergeant."

"Oh, I'm going to check and see because I have a feeling your liver looks like a raisin right now."

That was when Alibudbun came to the formation. He didn't have his smile, which was unusual. His forty soldiers were concerned now. Few things made Alibudbun frown and when it, did nobody liked the reason.

He stood in front of them and said, "Got some news I need to put out after revelry. Nobody goes anywhere until it is done."

That confused the Soldiers and the NCOs so instead of the usual banter before revelry, they were oddly quiet. When the horn went off and they saluted the flag, Alibudbun turned and said, "Okay, gather around."

They did, making a semi-circle. Jenny didn't like this. Alibudbun only did this when they messed up something or getting news they weren't going to like.

"Okay, guys," said Alibudbun, "going to get straight to the point. As of now, no cellphones will be brought to the field. All cellphones will be confiscated and stored in the arms room after weapons draw on Wednesday. Anyone caught with a cellphone will be punished under UCMJ. This includes soldiers, officers, and NCO's."

There was an uproar. People started yelling in protest.

"The fuck, man!" yelled Jackson.

"What am I supposed to do out there for two weeks, twiddle my thumbs?!" yelled Jobe, a fat guy with a mustache, who spent most of his time on his phone.

"I got bills to pay!" yelled Russel. "How am I supposed to call my daughter in Jamaica without my phone?"

Alibudbun raised his hands trying to restore order. "Listen. Listen!"

"Hey, shut up!" yelled Sergeant Hendrickson, an NCO of Second Squad; a skinny blonde Sergeant from Maryland. His voice was usually soft, but when it got commanding, you tended to listen.

"Thank you," said Alibudbun. "This is not coming from Lt. Perry or our Captain. Hell, not even our Battalion Commander. This is coming from Division. I know it's bullshit and we are trying to reverse it, but as of now, no cellphones. This doesn't mean leave them at home. It means you have to bring them in, hand them over, and that is the only way you're getting your weapon."

There were more dark murmurs which added up to a collective 'fuck this shit'.

CPL Pag, Sergeant Sengal, and Sergeant Garcia glared at their squad, a control in the chaos the other squads lacked.

"I know this is bull," said Alibudbun, "and we are fighting it, but just prepare yourselves for the worst, okay? That is all I ask."

There was a muttering of reluctant consent.

"Okay, Squad Leaders, take charge, conduct PT. Running."

His NCO's saluted and Alibudun joined the other Platoon Leaders and Sergeants for their PT session. Jenny wasn't happy about losing her phone. Hamish was frowning hard. Hickman, who learned they were running, thought, *ohh God*.

They went to stretch, Sergeant Garcia looked at her NCO's and soldiers and said, "I know this is stupid, but don't give up, okay? It's two weeks. Many of us have been overseas for over a year without talking to our fams for months at a time. We can do this, no problem. We are First Squad for a reason. We are the best, and we can handle the most. I won't have you guys just sitting around for nothing. Me and my two NCOs will come up with stuff, and we will have a great field. Besides, they didn't ban poker."

"Hooah!" yelled Jenny and the others, and they started PT.

When the run started, Hickman moaned, "She's trying to kill me."

Monday finished quickly and the soldiers headed home, except for Hamish. Hamish told Hickman he went to Bible study, which many believed, but in reality he was heading for Blairwood Meadows Apartments. As a consolation prize for losing their cellphones privileges during the field, he and the others got off work early to spend time with their families. He hated hiding things from Tone and Jenny, but this he kept very close to his heart, for if anyone were to discover what he was doing, he'd be worse than shunned from his community; he'd possibly be ostracized from his best friends.

He arrived in the car he bought a year ago. A Honda CR-V, small, fast, and nice, with a bit of cargo room to boot. He parked in the guest space, and after he got to the building, knocked on the door he intended to enter. The one he knocked on Sunday afternoon. Sergeant Garcia answered; she was dressed in a black robe. Her golden-brown highlighted hair was wet from a shower. She started to breathe hard in excitement. Her cleavage showing between the robe as it rose and fell with each breath. Because she was in an E-6 slot, she was given a waiver to live off post so sneaking around with her was easier than it would be to sneak around in the barracks. Hamish knew what they were doing was wrong. Both via military training and his Amish upbringing, but he couldn't help himself. He loved her.

He walked inside and Camila Garcia closed the door behind him. Once it was closed, Camila turned to Jacob Hamish who walked forward in his red t-shirt and jeans. His hand, going to the tied sash that held the robe together, unfastened it. Camila let it fall away, her tan body revealed. Jacob went to her and kissed her. She tugged at his shirt and let her take it off him; bending to help her with the difference in height. She jumped on to him and he carried her to the bedroom; her legs around his midriff, her hands around his neck.

This didn't happen day one. Garcia treated him like any other soldier. He respected her and obeyed her without question. Then a lunch happened in the chow hall. It had been a bad day and the two just talked about ways to improve morale. Then another; then ten more. Then one day they stopped. At work Jacob asked why when they were doing PMCS. Garcia explained she thought they were too close and needed some distance. Jacob understood and didn't want her to feel conflicted. That changed on March 23, 2020 when COVID hit. Hickman got drunk that day when everything closed and he was stuck. Jacob called Camila and she picked them up; grabbed

Hickman at Coleman's Bar and spent five hours getting him to bed. They stayed all night with him; the two sitting in the corner with each other. They started to talk. Talking turned to flirting then they kissed. That kiss turned to more than a kiss. Three months later they were married in a private ceremony. Hamish, knowing he would be a pariah, exiled from the Amish community because of this, decided it didn't matter. He loved her.

They couldn't be with each other as often as they would like. Jacob lived in the barracks; Camila was still an NCO and wasn't allowed relations with one of her soldiers. They couldn't admit they were married until he was done with his contract in seven months. If they did, they'd both be demoted and lose their jobs. That was the only reason why Camila slipped on a condom for Jacob, Hamish thought it was against both their religions. A baby would make matters more complicated than they needed it to be.

It would be over a week before he could make love with her again but at this moment, and on Sunday morning, through the evening, he needed her because of his brother and he needed his anchor. Needed, the reason he lived for, outside the Army and medical school. She held him, giving him the security he needed to go on with life.

Four condoms later and a morning after pill after later, they were both lying in bed, holding each other. Camila held Jacob, laying on his chest, hearing his heartbeat coming into her ear with regular thumps.

"I love you," said Jacob.

"I love you, too," responded Camila.

"How are you holding?"

"After the cellphone fiasco, I've been better."

"I wish," said Jacob, holding her hard the way she liked "I

could have helped you."

"I wish," said Camila, looking up and stroking his face "I could hold you during the field."

They held each other till three in the morning when Hamish drove home. Not knowing Jenny had seen his car as she drove back from her dance lessons.

CHAPTER SIX

Admissions and the Field

"Real love is to offer your life at the feet of another."

— John Ajvide Lindqvist *Let the Right One In*

Jenny was confused.

The Sunday lessons started fine, Jenny working with a partner. He was a handsome Greek guy named Adonis. And he was an Adonis. Black hair slicked back, olive skin, body chiseled out of stone, the kind to make a girl like Jenny want to be touched. Madam Roseta did this on purpose. She told Jenny she was going to have to learn to dance with dancers she didn't find as appealing as Adonis. But when you've never danced with a partner, it's best to learn with someone you're willing to let yourself go for; and let go she did. Realizing that she was willing to be lead, instead of just doing it by herself. Adonis lead; her natural talent, allowing her to claim a spotlight, but her movements were controlled by the strong handed Adonis.

When it was done, Roseta said she did great and Jenny felt like she was on top of the world. However, before going home she scheduled one more lesson for Monday evening, knowing she wasn't going to have a lot of time to dance in the field and having no cellphone was going to suck. Plus she wanted Adonis' hands on her again. They did another session on Monday evening and the dance was great, trying more complicated maneuvers this time. She struggled a little bit but she managed to find her footing thanks to Adonis. Adonis just had a way of making her feel alive, but at the same time, not in control of her body. It was strange, almost puppet like for Jenny, and yet feeling some control and comfort from Adonis.

After the lesson, she headed back home by cutting threw Black River near Sergeant Garcia's apartment. As she came towards it, she saw Hamish's CR-V. What was that doing there? Then, before she passed it, she saw the door open and Hamish went inside the apartment. That was something that made her almost turn around.

It could have meant anything she thought as she entered the base. He could have been going there to fill out some paperwork. He was being slotted for BLC. But no, Hamish only had seven months left and had stated he was more interested in starting medical school then BLC. *Sarg didn't treat him any differently than the rest of us;* she rationalized as she pulled up to an open parking spot at her barracks. *She treats him like everyone else. She treats him like a soldier. But what if she didn't? Were there any moments that pointed to a relationship? When Hamish talked to her about his brother; had? She did just, for a moment, she touched his arm.*

So what? Jenny continued thinking. *Why should I care? She isn't showing favoritism. Why should I give a fuck? Hamish is your friend and your battle. He's like a brother to you. You at least owe him the fact that you know, or suspect.*

She decided that and headed upstairs. Instead of going to her room, she went to Hamish and Hickman's door and was about to knock when she realized he probably wasn't home yet. She would set her alarm for early, maybe 0500, and go to his room then. She went back to her room showered and went to bed.

She woke up five and a half hours later, showered, changed, and went to Hamish and Hickman's room and knocked. She kept knocking until a red eyed Hickman answered. His ebony skin seemed lighter, almost sickly.

"Jenny," he asked, "what time is it?"

"A little after five. Is Hamish home?"

"Hamish left last night." murmured Hickman, looking at his watch. "Oh, yeah, Bible study."

"I need to talk to him. How sober are you?"

"Enough to know this is serious."

He turned to his right and knocked on Hamish's door. There was a moan then, "What? Room inspection?"

"Nah, man, Jenny is here."

"Hickman? Why are you up before I am?"

"Because of Jenny."

Hamish opened his door and seeing Jenny said, "What's wrong?"

Jenny stepped forward and whispered in his ears three words, "You and Garcia."

Hamish's eyes widened and realizing what was going on looked at Hickman, who looked ready to die for the second time this week, and said, "Hickman, can you get us some coffee?"

"We have coffee?" asked Hickman, his eyes bulging.

"I have some instant."

"Shit," muttered Hickman. Then, in a southern accented voice dripping in sarcasm said, "Yes, master, right away, master. Dick, what am I, a butler?"

He left and Hamish ushered Jenny into his room. She sat on one of the two seats and Hickman on the bed. They waited in silence for ten minutes then Hickman came in holding three mugs and handed them out. He sat on the second chair and took a sip; the warm liquid doing wonders for him, bringing the ebony back to his skin. Jenny told Hamish what she saw. Hamish listened to the whole explanation before answering.

"I was there," he said. "Not for paperwork. I went there because she is my wife."

Hickman sprayed coffee across the room. The words hit him like a battering ram.

"Your what?!" he yelled.

Jenny stared. "You're married to her and you didn't tell us?"

"It wasn't supposed to happen." said Hamish and he explained the situation leading to his marriage to Sergeant Garcia. They listened and the pieces fell into place.

"How long you been hitched?" asked Hickman.

"Six months."

"Wait," said Jenny, "both you and Sergeant Garcia went on leave in February, did you...?"

"We were on our honeymoon in Vermont."

"Holy shit," said Hickman, staring at the coffee, "no wonder she was in a good mood."

"Don't you dare," snapped Hamish, "she is still our Sergeant."

Hickman looked down, ashamed. "Sorry man."

"I know it is wrong," Hamish said. "But I'm out in a few months. Please, don't take this away from her. You both respect her. She has helped us; we owe her that much."

Jenny looked down, knowing her answer. But she had to ask him something, something she couldn't let go.

"What about your community?" she asked, "What will they say?"

"I will be shunned," he said, "exiled for all time. I could still be a doctor for them, but no longer Amish. I love her, and that is all that matters. I can accept being separated from my community, but not from her."

"Damn," said Hickman, "you love her a lot, don't you?"

"I do."

"I won't say anything," said Jenny, putting her hand on his, "I love you like a brother; I can't betray you."

"Hell," said Hickman, "I won't say shit. Just promise you will take care of her."

"I will," said Hamish.

They got to PT at 0620, and Sergeant Garcia marched up to them at the field, pissed they were later than usual.

"What the fuck? I told you all, fifteen minutes prior. What took you so long?"

Jenny, who was the spokesperson for their group said simply, "Hamish's relationship problems."

Confusion hit Garcia's face, then understanding, then fear, then acceptance.

"Are you going..."

"You are our Sergeant," said Hickman, "as long as you're willing to Article 15 his ass on a drug bust, we don't care."

"You don't have to worry," said Jenny, "we won't betray

you."

Garcia relaxed and said, looking at Hamish, speaking in a quiet whisper, "Good, because I love him."

Hamish mouthed, "I love you, too."

"PT time!" yelled Garcia, going back to full metal jacket. "Then we get ready for the field."

***

Orson found it at 0500. The basket left in front of a half burned down house in LeRay. It was wicker and brown, but what was inside was toxic. It was toxic to his kind. He didn't understand why, not even the Elder who lived with man since the Stone Age, why the contents were so poisonous to vampires. Inside were ten cloves of garlic and a silver chain, six feet long. Along with that, a lock and key.

The basket was dreadful to touch, but touch he must, for that would seal the plan. Once he had it, there was no turning back. He reached out, his hand trembling, and grabbed the basket's handle, and zipped back to the nest. Thank you, General Bryant.

He zips back to the nest, only an hour and a half before sunrise, the basket coved by aluminum foil. When he returned, all his brethren were snug in their coffins, including Lee-Arne, who feared silver more than anything, having been cut by it years ago.

He zipped past them until he reached Legwang's dried up husk, revealing his fangs at it, daring the meditative bastard to challenge what he was doing. Legwang didn't react, as usual. Orson walked into the elder's chamber and saw the large eight-foot coffin leaning on the wall. He smiled.

So long we have feed on the weak, you have forgotten what it is like to be strong, thought Orson, as he stepped forward, excited over the prospect of feed on clean blood; - not homeless. He squatted down, dropping the basket and removed the foil. A pair of rubber gloves were on top of it and he put them on. He was so frightened when he touched the garlic. However, he needed to know if he could with the thick, black, rubber gloves. He touched it with the tip of his clawed forefinger. It didn't hurt or burn him, his flesh was protected by the rubber.

Smiling, he gratefully put on his mask, pulled up the strings of garlic and went to the coffin. His hands were shaking, knowing what he was planning to do was sacrilegious, but it had to be done for the clan. His hand grabbed the lid of the box, hoping against hope that the Elder slept. As he lifted the lid of the coffin, he was scared his head was going to be separated from his body as the wooden box creaked open.

The Elder slept, in the sleep of death which all vampires knew to be natural. Removing the chain from the basket, he poured the garlic into the Elder's coffin. He then slammed it shut with a resounding boom. Then, grabbing the chain, he wrapped it around the coffin, three coils worth and put the lock between the two ends. Silver wouldn't break under a vampires touch, even as the Elder started to bang on the top of his coffee, screaming at the smell of the garlic, unable to move because of the silver.

Orson hissed down the hall, and out of the shadows, three more vampires, including Lee-Arne, and two more ivory skinned vampires, Cain and Maguri, both male when they were human, and helped lift the heavy coffin of the Elder. The coffin alone wasn't the problem, it was the great power dying inside it, screaming, and cursing in some guttural dead language, shaking the coffin, making it hard to carry. They got to the mouth of the cave, and looked down to the river below, the Elder roaring like a lion. Orson hissed and the group threw the coffin into the river. It flowed, half submerged, down the wate, and after a bend, it was out of sight.

Orson looked up, the sun coming soon, looking over his shoulder, and nodding to the other three, all of them turning and resting. Soon, tomorrow night, the night hunt would start; the first in decades. It took a long time to convince the others during tonight's hunt. Most were still against this, having been decades since they hunted a large party of humans at once. Many were fearful. But they won't break ranks, for now, Orson was the Elder. Tired, he went to sleep in his dirt and coffin.

Meanwhile, in the far end of the cave, the mummified husk of Legwang opened his dry eyes. His dried, almost papery skin made many in the clan believe he was dead. But he was not dead. He was enlightened. He knew the history of the world, his knowledge only second to another, older being. His being, like himself, knew why the vampires had to survive, even if they could only feed on the edges of humanities huge population. The ancient ley lines were awakening again. The plague had lessened their hold on the world. The black plague, which had killed almost all of the ancient power, was once known as magic. Though children5 of this great power, they were spared the purge of magic due to their nature. The twelve elders, knowing that more death would come, swore to, along with other survivors, to hide and wait. Now, this child, Orson, would soon risk not only his clan, but the elven others. He couldn't stand against their unity and would have to help. In the end, weather this hunt would be successful or not, it was his duty to preserve the clan, and search for the Elder at night. Let the others have their fun. As long as the Elder survived, it ensured their line would not die.

These children would soon learn why the vampires had to stay at the edges of humanity. They would kill almost all of them, but soon they would learn why humans were so successful at killing their kind. They might win, but many would die. Many more than they planned. And, when he found the Elder, he would teach these children true fear. But for now, he had to wait, and watch, as he always had since the beginning of his life.

For the first time in decades he moved; his old bones creaking under dead flesh. He stood; knowing daylight was only a half hour away and zipped out. He found who he was looking for in seconds. It was the old man who walked his dog every day near the clan's cave at sunrise. They were going to have to move the clan soon, and this hunt the children of the night were planning would force this move faster. But for now, he must be as strong as he could.

The old man of eighty, who walked a little poodle, couldn't react as Legwang zipped in front of him, killing the dog and biting the man's neck before he could scream. The old man's eyes built in terror as he watched that of Legwang, once looking like a mummy, slowly puffing up like a puffer fish, turning into what looked like a beautiful, naked, teenage boy of seventeen, ivory skin, pointed ears, black eyes, black, long hair, yet oddly feminine features. Though he looked young, Legwang, having been born in the eastern lands before China was China, was one of the most respected vampires of the ages outside the Elder. He had survived for 12,000 years and watched the rise and fall of civilizations of the old, now extinct Magic Users, to humanity's current age.

When he was done with the man, he ran with the two corpses three miles into the woods, dumped the bodies, and zipped back. His naked body, glowing, felt the sun come closer.

He got back to the cave in time. He picked up his clothing, a tie-dyed shirt from burning man, blue Elvis pants, and running shoes. One must have his modesty. He went to his coffin, opened it, and sunk into the dirt and slept. His work began tomorrow.

CHAPTER SEVEN

The Field

"Those who were massacred fled their way. They fled towards something that was beyond; heaven or in the worst case, eternal darkness. They were the lucky ones because those left behind are in hell. "

- Steve Niles, *30 Days of Night, Vol. 1*

Jenny arrived at the company at 0530 as instructed for weapons draw. As also ordered, she had her cellphone in her pocket. All her gear was in her locker, put there the day before. Shirts, underwear, green and brown shocks, boots, a knife, an E-tool, ballistic glasses, hydration kit, PTs to sleep in, fleece, IOTV, some books, and Kevlar, all ready to go.

She got in line with Hamish and Hickman, Jackson currently at the front, handing his cellphone over under the watchful eyes of the Platoon Sergeants and Lt. Perry, their Platoon Leader. He was only six months out of West Point, but already showed to be a capable commander. He was smart, kind, cunning, and one hell of a PT stud. This was hidden under a tall, gangly appearance, glasses, and a teenaged looking face.

"They're really doing this," muttered Hickman as Jackson finally got his weapon, and had an angry look on his face, his phone no longer in hand. Sergeant Miller, Third Platoon, Third Squad, came up next and though not looking happy, stayed professional, and handed in his phone, signed for his weapon, his phone put into a box and taken away. He was pissed, having a newborn baby he wasn't going to see at all, even on video phone.

"This is going to be a miserable two weeks," whispered Jenny.

"I admit," said Hamish, "even I don't like this and I rarely use my phone."

"Ain't going to be fully boring," smiled Hickman.

Both soldiers looked at him as he mouthed, "Jack Daniels."

"You didn't," whispered Jenny.

"One quart canteen worth of it," whispered Hickman.

"Sergeant Garcia is right," said Hamish, though he was smiling, "you do have a problem."

All three chuckled, but the two were grateful to Hickman for bending a rule. Sergeant Garcia came up to them, and they all went to parade rest for her, the OCP going on to their chest as their hands went behind their back.

"Okay," she said, "let's see them."

While they all knew there had been a change in the way they all looked at each other, their respect for her was still there, and thus they pulled out their cellphones. She nodded, and said, "Good."

They continued in the line until they went to get their weapons. Inside the arms room, PFC Delacruz, a short Caribbean woman, dark of skin and wearing glasses, gave them a form. When Jenny got hers, a DA form 2062 she signed for a M4, ACOG sights, and night vision goggles. When she get the items, after taking note of the weapon's stock, Delacruz handed her a second DD214, took a note on what type of cellphone Jenny had, gave the form to Jenny and said, "Don't lose it."

She then put the cellphone in a small box, wrote 'Jenny Dang, SPC, First Squad, Third Platoon, weapon number 34' on the top box. Then she put it in the slot of the weapons locker where she got Jenny's weapon, overseen by Captain Timothy, the Company Commander. While any NCO would have watched this, the Commander, knowing how unfair this situation was to the troops, took it upon himself to ensure that the personal property of the soldiers would be secured. He was a medium sized Arnold Schwarzenegger looking guy, with a large mole on the side of his neck. His brown eyes followed each box containing a cellphone. Had Delacruz open it for his personal inspection, ensuring the phone was there. Then, once closed, put to pieces of tape on two sides of the box, then watched Delacruz place it in the weapon lockers.

First Sergeant Michael, also close by, ensured that the soldier handling the cellphones stayed honest about her work. Both they and the XO would have the keys of the lockers with them once everyone would have their weapons drawn, to ensure no phones were lost to this stupid order they received. They knew they were asking a lot of their soldiers, and while unfair, it had to be obeyed. However, doing it this way they would keep the soldiers trust, no matter what.

Jenny joined the others at the locker, pulled out her ruck, assault pack, IOTV, and Kevlar, putting them on her body. She and her two best friends joined the rest of First Squad outside with PVT Jackson, PFC Sosa, Sergeant Sengal, CPL Pag, and Sergeant Garcia. After a quick inspection, she went to a box of MREs and said let them know it was breakfast.

"No hot chow?" asked Jackson, his large body sagging.

"No time. Load up."

They all muttered grumpily but did as they were told. They went to the convoy, were LMTVs, HMMV's, a few Wreckers, tool trucks, trailers, a mobile kitchen, and a couple of Water Buffalos would transport the troops weapons, food, medication, shelters, generators, heaters and bullets needed to complete the mission. There were over a 115 vehicles in all going to the field and First Squad loaded on to their LMTV, Second joining them as well. Before loading, they were given four megs of ammo. Two were blanks, two live. The Ammo truck was going to be delayed but, they would have enough for the exercise tomorrow.

"Well," said Jackson as they all took their seats, "this is going to suck."

Sosa said, "Two weeks without my wife's sexy body. Ay Dios Mío, how will I survive?"

"Well," said Hickman, "time for a nap. Three hours then set up; better get some rest."

Even Jenny thought that was brilliant. As soon as SFC Alibudbun confirmed with Lt. Perry that all were accounted for, the truck was closed, sealing Jenny and the others inside for the three-hour drive. What none of them knew was that someone came last night and put a single drop of blood on every vehicle in the motorpool. That blood was strong, and for the creatures of the night, it would be like a signal flare. Three hours later, Jenny was awakened by the ten o'clock sun; the LMTV was opened by Sergeant Garcia. Site Indigo, nothing but an open field surrounded by a tree line about a half a mile away. Big, and boring, designed to isolate and keep soldiers as far away from civilizations as they could manage.

"Let's go!" Sergeant Garcia yelled, "Need to start setting up."

They unloaded, Jenny, Hamish, and Hickman going to the truck that had the tent, the generator, and the heater.

"Let's do this!" yelled Alibudbun with a wide grin, walking up to the group, "I want us set up in an hour and cots inside before 1300."

They worked like army ants, and Third had their tent up before First, Second and Fourth platoon. Within two hours, the generator was hooked up, the heater was ready, and the forty cots were inside the large, dark green, camo covered tent. Their gear was put up, and soon, they were all relaxing their tense muscles. Jenny put her cot next to Hamish and Hickman's; Jackson and Sosa across from them. Sergeant Garcia was on the far side with the other NCOs, Lt. Perry at the front.

"Well," said Alibudbun, "quick note, guard starts at 2000 tonight. Jackson, Jobe, you're up first. Jenny, Russel, you got it after at 2200."

"Damn it," muttered Jobe, his solemn face looking even more miserable without his phone.

"Roger," said the rest.

"Get some rest." SFC Alibudbun said. "We hit the ground hard tomorrow."

"Hooah!" yelled Third Squad, as they pulled out an old iPod for music and movies or books.

"Man," said Hickman, "this is going to be boring."

Hamish, who snuck a glance at Garcia, who secretly returned it, said, "I have a few books."

"Fuck your religious text." Hickman looked over and saw

Hamish holding out a copy of World War Z. "On the other hand," he laughed, taking it, "who says a little religion can't open your eyes."

"Told you he'd ended up eating his words." said Jenny with a grin. She closed her eyes.

The TOC tent, code name ECP Forward for the mission, was the heart of every field operation. It was where Lt. Colonel Swarts slept, commanded, and operated from with his XO, Major Dong, and his Command Sergeant Major, CSM Dickerson, operated the field. All three were inside right now, making damn sure that all the radios were working. The ones at the guard post were, as were all the local ones, and the Chaplin's personal one we're all online. Now to test the long range one as SSG Helden contacted Fort Drum via rear guard staff duty.

"549, this is ECP Forward, can you read us."

Lt. Colonel Swarts bit his lip. He still hated this no cellphone bullshit, so he was going to make damn sure their communication was clear. At 55 years old, white hair, and battle scar, he was getting long in the tooth to be a Battalion Commander. But he loved it. He loved being the center, the go to man, to make this military machine work. Still, this situation was unfair to his soldiers. He was going make damn sure if anything happened to the soldiers or their families, they were able to get them out fast. FRG would be in constant contact as well, ready with Red Cross messages if they came in. The response came in, and Swarts was able to breathe again when he heard the words.

"ECP Forward, this is 549, read you loud and clear."

CSM Dickerson, a woman of forty-nine, African American, and lovely, smiled for the first time in hours. She was a hard woman, but a great SGM. Firm but compassionate.

Major Dong, formerly of the South Korean Army but now a

full citizen of the United States, smiled as well.

"Roger will make contact every hour." said SSG Helden

"Roger," said 549 staff duty NCOIC, "careful out there."

"Roger out."

Lt. Colonel Swarts nodded, pleased, turning to the SGM and said, "Keep me updated on any developments."

"Yes, sir." said SGM Dickerson.

"Anything for tomorrow, sir?" asked Major Dong.

"Zero 600 wake up. The 514 will go to the range as soon as the ammo truck arrives."

"Yes, sir."

"Ensure all guards are posted at 2200 hours. Then get some sleep."

"Yes, sir."

Swarts sighed. Well, they did it, and the camp was set up no problem. It was going to be a good night, he felt it. The thing about everything going smoothly was that, when it did, something was bound to happen, and at 2245, it would be a big thing.

***

Orson looked through the shadows, seeing the lights from the tent bright against the night sky. So much they relied on this technology; so long they used it to conquer the world. It would be a hindrance, but not a deadly one.

Orson was shaking with excitement. The smell of the fresh, clean, untainted blood of these soldiers was mouthwatering. Only a few of the soldiers were spoiled with alcohol and tobacco, but it was better than the meth, heroine, and oxy, which made him so sick. Even those in the clan who were reluctant to participate in this feeding couldn't deny this. Lee-Arne stood next to him; her obsidian skin made her almost invisible in the shadows. She stood there, smiling, anticipating the feeding that was to come, as were most of the others. Legwang stood on the other side of him. Orson had been surprised the old husk had awakened for this. It also still surprised him how young the vampire looked, barely in his late teens when he was turned by the Elder. Unlike the others, who stood, excited for the meal, Legwang seemed almost pensive, relaxed.

"Thought you be excited for a new meal," said Orson to him.

Legwang turned, his beautiful face cracking into a smile that made Orson uneasy. "Blood should not be the focus of one's once immortal existence," said Legwang, "I awake to only help the clan, not to indulge in frivolous activities."

"You will be eating your words old man," said Orson, his fangs showing.

Legwang shrugged. His long brown hair was in a ponytail. Vampires did have hair, but if they wanted to keep it, they could never shave it. Their hair remained the same throughout their lives. Orson had shaven his away, finding it was easier to clean himself in the night. Some of the males did the same, but none of the female vampires did. It was a fashion choice. Two of the vamps with them even had beards. One vamp, a former Olympic athlete, a woman by the name of Shumi, still had the pubic hair she had when she died. Orson found it strange, but like the others, didn't ask her about it.

He turned to the forty-one vampires assembled, and said, "Vehicles and radios tonight. Feed if you get a chance but destroy their transportation and communication first. We will feed on them tomorrow until we are full."

They nodded.

Orson started to lead them. Tonight, the natural order will be discovered. Vampires will once again rule the night, the other twelve clans would soon follow his example. Tonight, so much fun was going to happen.

CHAPTER EIGHT

Night Zero

"And then suddenly he was there, charging down the hallway

like death in a cowboy duster."

— Richelle Mead, *Vampire Academy*

Jackson and Jobe sat out in the cold at the constructed Guard Station Two. They had their rifles, NVG's, and a small, green, Army radio, and were as bored as hell. Jobe, at this point, would be playing on his phone. Jackson would be, too. Two hours of nothing to do. Fuck this shit. Nothing to see but the C-wire twenty feet ahead of them that surrounded the camp and the black tree line, and the full moon, which, at this moment, was covered by clouds.

"Why are we even out here?" asked Jobe, his unsmiling fat face staring off into the night.

"Well," said Jackson who was a tiny bit more professional than Jobe, though not by much, in his own words, "we have to do it anyway; down range."

"We're not down range," grumbled Jobe, one nearly closed eye somehow managing to glare at Jackson.

Jackson shrugged, his IOTV helping keep to a little warmth on this chilled autumn night.

"This phone thing is bullshit." grumbled Jobe. "What was the brass thinking?"

"Probably nothing." responded Jackson with a chuckle. "Logic: the enemy of the military."

"What a surprise," grumbled Jobe, one hand supporting his head.

Jackson shook his head, turning back to the tree line.

"Hey, there's someone... no, two people ahead. Right before the tree line."

Jobe raised his head, and opened his eyes, first time showing something other than contempt on his face. Perhaps it was faint interest, or annoyance, Jackson couldn't tell. They both pulled out their NVGs, and in the green hue, saw them. Two figures in hoodies and jeans; standing off about four hundred yards away.

"Well," said Jobe, glumly, "so much for sleep."

Jackson pulled out his M4 and yelled, "You in the tree line identify yourself!"

Nothing, though some movement from 514's other platoon's guard post. The voice drew interest in the still night air.

"What a surprise," said Jobe, sarcastically, not moving his own fat ass in any way to get his rifle. "They don't answer."

"Call it up," whispered Jackson, holding up his rifle under their makeshift shelter of plywood, tent stakes, and camo netting.

Grumbling, Jobe grabbed the radio, his NVG over his right eye, observing the two figures before them. Grabbing the receiver, shaped like an old-time telephone, he spoke into it, pressing the button on the side, talking into it with little interest.

"ECP Forward, ECP Forward, this is Guard Post 2, do you read?"

A moment of static, then, "Guard Post 2, this is ECP Forward, we read you, go ahead."

"Possible hostiles on the outer perimeter of the C-Wire. Number of hostiles: two. Uniform: hoodies, and jeans. Weapons..."

That's when Jobe realized, there were no weapons, not even those fake, rubber AK's the brass sometimes brought out.

"Guard Post 2, you still there?"

"Stand by, ECP," said Jobe, and turned to Jackson, his weapon raised and full of blanks.

"Jackson, they don't have weapons."

Jackson looked up with his own NVG connected to his Kevlar. He was right. No weapons at all. During training, there were always a few running around at night, guys acting as bad guys. Sometimes they wore civilians, but they always carried some weapon, real or fake.

"Civilians, way out here?"

Jobe got back on the radio.

"ECP Forward, there are no weapons on the hostiles. Zero weapons. Possible civilians. Need confirmation."

"Stand by," said the ECP Forward radio operator.

Jobe then turned to Jackson, "Get CPL Pag."

Jackson nodded, got up and left. Jobe, feeling nervous, grabbed his carbine. He hoped this was training and not something else. Though, for some odd reason, he thought that wasn't going to be the case tonight. "Should've stayed at home," he muttered.

The clouds continued to move across the sky. The moon would soon reveal the hostiles.

SSG Helden turned to a short, beer bellied Second Lieutenant, "Sir, Guard Post 2 is reporting hostiles."

The Lieutenant turned as did the Lt. Colonel, who was reading a book who looked up in confusion.

"Hostiles?" he asked, his eyes showing incomprehension.

"Yes, sir, they..."

Lt. Colonel Swarts went over to his XO and CSM and shook them awake.

"Either of you order any incursion teams tonight without my say so?"

They shook their heads. That made Swarts brows raise.

"Sir," said SSG Helden, "I'm getting similar reports from Guard Post 1, 6, and 10... and, God, too much chatter I can't get through."

The command team stood. Something wasn't right.

CPL Pag was dreaming of Pizza Hut when Jackson grabbed his shoulders and shook him awake, saying softly, "Corporal, Corporal."

CPL Pag opened his eyes, "What?"

"We got possible hostiles, Corporal. But I don't think their training actors." explained Jackson.

"What?"

"Just come with me."

"Jackson, if this is some bullshit, I swear to God I'm going to shoot you."

"Come on."

CPL Pag dragged his ass out of his cot, threw on his gear and boots, and went with Jackson. They got to Guard Post 2, and Pag saw this wasn't a joke because it looked like Jobe was giving a shit. When Jobe gave a shit about something other than his cellphone, you knew something was going on. Pulling down his NVG connected to the front of his Kevlar, he looked ahead of him and saw about seven personnel in front of the wood line.

"Five more joined our friends," confirmed Jobe, still speaking in the radio, and cursing when he wasn't able to get through. Pag felt his stomach drop. What the hell was this?

"Identify yourselves!" he yelled to the group. They didn't respond.

"What is ECP saying?" asked Jackson.

"I can't get through," said Jobe in unsettling frustration, a rare tone for Jobe.

Pag looked out, removing his NVGs from his eye, just as the moon was freed from the clouds. At that same moment, as the moon light made the group shine, the people beyond the C-wire lowered their hoods and two more joined the seven, making their numbers nine. What Pag saw made him feel uneasy.

"Fuck," gasped Jackson, his carbine raised in fear, "Those are some pale mother fuckers."

"Some are black as fuck," said Jobe, now standing as well, the radio forgotten, his rifle in hand.

"Fall back," said Pag, "I'm not liking this."

They started to back up when an unearthly scream broke the night. It was like cutting metal mixed with a Tasmanian devil's call. It was loud and hit the three like a knife. Then the group before them, and before the other posts, started moving forward. At first, they walked, then they started to jog.

"Fire blanks!" yelled Pag, raising his own rifle. Jackson and Jobe raised theirs as well and fired. The shots echoed through the field, but it didn't scare them, they just started to go faster until they were at a run.

They leapt, the first to reach the C-Wire, sailing right over it, over twenty feet in the air, and landed in the camp, then, almost faster than the human eye could track, five zipped away to the camp's center.

"Switch to live rounds!" yelled Pag.

"CPL," said Jackson, "I don't think that's legal."

"Fuck legalities, shoot them."

Jackson dropped his blank mag and reached for his live ammo when something landed to his left. He had time to see it. Its black eyes, fangs, obsidian skin, pointed ears, and corn rolls. The smell of earth hit Jackson's nose like a freight train. It stuck out an arm, hitting Jackson's right shoulder, sending him flying and landing five feet short of the C-Wire. He landed with a gasp, but didn't have time to think, the creature was upon him, its mouth full of razor sharp teeth. Jackson screamed as it seemed ready to go for his throat.

Three shots rang out, live rounds, hitting the obsidian thing in the chest, and it fell over, growling clutching its side. Pag flew over Jackson, landing on top of the creature, punching its face twice, and Jackson scramble back to his feet, grabbing his M4 as he did. He stood, Jobe and him raising their rifles, when the heard the sounds of screams from the camp, causing them to turn, and go pale with fear.

CPL Pag was going for a final punch when he saw the creature below him smiling, the sounds of screams and metal ripping around them, then Pag felt something hit his chest, sending him flying backwards, landing on his back. Then the creature was on top of him, Pag crossing his arms over himself, trying to keep the creature away, but feeling, despite his effort, it was for nothing. It slowly coming down to him, almost teasingly, knowing Pag's defiance was pointless. Pag looked back and yelled, "Jackson, Jobe, run!"

They didn't need to be told twice as the creature sunk its fangs into Pag's neck, drinking his blood.

Lt. Colonel Swarts heard the scream, then the gunfire, SSG Helden trying to get info on the radio.

"I'm going out there," Colonel Swarts said, as his XO and CSM joined him.

Before they could get out, something came in out of nowhere, blocking their exit. It was ivory skinned, had spikey hair, a nose ring, a leather jacket with spikes on the shoulders. All the three of them saw were the fangs in its mouth, clawed hands, black eyes, and pointed ears. It smiled, showing its sharp teeth, then its hands went out, sending the Colonel flying, hitting his head on the tent pole, nearly dislodging it, sending him into unconscious.

The thing then grabbed both the XO and the CSM's by their faces, and sent them flying, their bodies landing in an entangled heap. It then zipped forward, grabbed SSG Helden's neck, the force breaking the neck with an audible crack, drinking his blood. Once done, the creature went for the radio, balling its clawed hand into a fist, and slamming it down, the radio shattering under his blow. Then it zipped out, the command team slowly regaining their awareness, trying to figure out what just happened.

Jenny was shaken awake by Garcia, her face having a set look of controlled confusion at her squad leader's panicked face.

"Wake up SPC Dang. Hamish, Sosa, Hickman, get your asses up. This isn't a joke."

Jenny raised herself off her cot.

"What's..."

"No time," snapped Sergeant Garcia, "grab your gear and carbines. Don't worry about you're OCP tops. Move."

They did, putting on their gear, Jenny barely seeing Jobe and Jackson talking to the platoon leadership. Jenny didn't bother with her OCP top, just threw on her IOTV and Kevlar and ran outside with the others. All she saw was chaos. Screams, yelling, blood, and broken metal covered the ground. She saw soldiers fighting pale and dark figures, some ten at a time against one of these figures, but they were sent flying like they were sacks of potatoes.

Lt. Perry came running out and yelled, "First Squad, SFC Alibudbun, with me, protect the trucks! Second, Third and Fourth Squad, protect the camp! Everyone, move!"

They moved. Lt. Perry, SFC Alibudbun lead the remaining First Squad to the trucks, nearly getting hit as the bodies of two soldiers flew past, landing in bloody heaps. The sound of live rounds being fired and the screams of the creatures broke out through the night. Then they saw it. An ivory colored creature with pointed ears, black eyes, and sharp claws, was at their trucks. It had ripped through all five of Third Platoon's vehicles, gas tanks and air collectors lying on the ground. The grass, it being soaked in oil, tires popped, and the rubber torn. Now, it was slashing at the last HMMV.

"Open fire, live rounds!" yelled Lt. Perry.

Jenny and the others loaded and opened fire. The creature, seeing this, ducked, the bullets missed him. Then, almost as if it teleported, it was in front of them. Perry and Alibudbun were thrown aside, flying away in opposite directions. Sergeant Garcia and Sergeant Sengel fired at this humanoid monster, but it grabbed the barrels of their rifles and tossed them, and the NCOs they were connected to, aside; the bullets missing the mark. Hickman tried to raise his weapon to rifle butt the thing, but he was swatted aside like a fly, knocked to the ground, unconscious.

This left Jenny, Sosa, Hamish, and Jackson, carbines raised, backing up as the creature smiled, then it zipped forward, grabbing both Jackson and Hamish. Jenny fell backwards, tripping on something that rolled under her foot, her M4 falling from her hand. She grabbed the thing that tripped her by instinct, realizing by feel it was a tent stake; a three foot piece of wood, and the end had snapped, revealing splinters.

Jackson was sent in the direction of the C-wire, and Hamish was sent flying into the air, his body breaking through the canvas of Third Platoon's tent, leaving a Bugs Bunny style hole, his arms and legs clearly outlined. Sosa tried to fire at it, but got kicked in the stomach, sent flying, her body tumbling backward and landing in the grass fifteen feet away. Then the creature turned to Jenny, and it smiled, shark teeth revealed behind his lips. Jenny's stomach dropped upon seeing those teeth, mixed with the dead black eyes. The ivory thing looked like a living corpse, a demon almost. Its predatory, powerful features stared at her with a deep, unending hunger, that was only ever sated but never satisfied, and she was the tool to be used for this sating and she believed it. The fear Jenny felt was a physical thing and she felt the blood flowing through her body, pulsing against her skin, even behind her eyes. Hot sweat came from every pore, and it took everything to control the function of her bladder staring at those dead eyes.

"No!" she screamed.

By instinct, she raised what remained of the stake in front of her, her eyes closed, praying. Then she felt something hit her, a great weight, almost dislodging the stake in her hands. She opened her eyes. The creature was inches away from her, its dark eyes bulging, mouth open, sharp fangs glaring from an opened, shocked mouth. Then she looked down. The creature had impaled itself in the heart on the stake; it penetrated its bone, some of the wood breaking but the rest cutting through, black blood dripping from the wound. For a long moment, it seemed paralyzed, and then it became a dead weight, the body going limp. It was dead.

She forced the creature off her and stood, and ran to Jackson, disgusted by the dark blood on her armored vest, scooping up her M4 as she ran. She got to Jackson, whose eyes were open, staring at the stars.

"Jackson, you okay?"

"Considering this is the second time I went flying tonight against my will, I'm surprise I am not feeling more pain."

Jenny laughed, adrenaline, fear and disbelief broke her mind, and she looked back at the corpse of the thing that had tried to kill her. She helped Jackson up, and they heard moans. Sosa came up, her IOTV shattered, the armor inside broken. She was gasping.

"I'm going to sue someone," she gasped, almost waddling, "I didn't sign on for this bullshit."

Jenny chuckled at that when another moan came. It was Hickman. Sosa pulled off her useless body armor and all three ran to him.

"Hickman?" asked Jenny, looking down at him as she joined Sosa at his side. A bruise was forming on his left cheek and one of his eyes were purpling as well, forming a thick bruise.

"Mofo broke my jaw," he said, not knowing that his jaw was intact. Jenny felt it, nothing out of place.

"You got lucky, it didn't."

"What the fuck was that thing? It swatted me like I was nothing but a damned horse fly."

Jackson and Sosa helped him into a sitting position, Hickman still in a daze. He blinked and saw the corpses of the creature, the thing on its back, the tent stake in its heart.

"All things considered, I'm in better shape than that piece of shit thing."

Sergeant Garcia and Sengel limped up. Sengel cracked his neck, Garcia circled her shoulders. Their rifle barrels were bent upwards.

"You all okay?" asked Sengel in his thick accent.

"Sore," said Hickman.

"Been better," said Jackson.

"IOTV is trashed," said Sosa.

"I'm okay," said Jenny.

Garcia's eyes widened, "Where is Hamish?"

"He..." began Jenny but was interrupted by another scream that came through the night. Jenny looked to her left and saw something by the tree line shining through the moon light. It was tiny at this distance, but Jenny had no doubt it was one of those creatures. Dozens of other screams were added to the din, soldiers pausing in the fight, trying to figure out what the hell is going on.

Then the buzzing sound. All the remaining creatures, which were minus the one Jenny killed, zipped back, heading to the tree line. They paused where the one that called them was standing, and Jenny thought there were over forty. Then they disappeared to the trees. Jenny and the remains of First Squad stared as they were soon joined by Lt. Perry and SFC Alibudbun, watching the creatures go. For a long moment nothing but the silence of the night.

Garcia asked again, her voice desperate, "Where is Hamish?"

Jenny stood and pointed to the tent. Seeing the hole and the light coming from it, Sergeant Garcia ran, running to the front entrance. The others followed, Sosa helping Hickman, who was still in a daze. Garcia got in first, Jenny right behind. Hamish was inside, his body landing on SPC Groves' bunk, landing on top of his sleeping bag, his arms and head hanging off one end of the bunk, his legs off another, legs bent on the ground. His rifle had landed two bunks ahead.

"Hamish!" screamed Garcia, and she ran to him, going to her knees with her hands on him, not hands of an Army NCO, but that of a wife, begging is he still alive. He was, he moaned, his Kevlar on the ground, its straps breaking via the force of impact. Slowly, he came back to life.

"Oh, thank god," she moaned, hugging him.

"You okay?" asked Jenny, getting to his head. He looked up.

"What the hell was that?" he asked, his voice thick with pain. Both Jenny and Garcia laughed, both realizing that Hamish, up until then, had never sworn before.

"Don't know baby," said Garcia, helping him up, "Don't..."

The tent flap opened and Alibudbun came in and seeing Hamish rushed over and asked if he was okay.

"I'm a little bit dazed," muttered Hamish. This caused them all to laugh.

Lt. Perry came in but was followed by the others. Hamish sat on the bunk, Jenny and Sergeant Garcia taking off his armor and examining him.

"I'm okay," said Hamish, embarrassed by all the attention.

Perry turned to Alibudbun and said, "Check on the other squads. See if we lost anyone else. I want figures as soon as possible."

"Yes, sir," said Alibudbun.

"First Squad, rest for now, now that is an order."

"Yes, sir," they all said, and he left.

When he was gone, Garcia turned to Hickman, who was holding his head, and said, "Hickman, get that stash of booze I know you have. That's an order."

"What?" Hickman looked up.

"You heard me."

Hickman smiled and said, "Yes, Sergeant."

He went to his assault pack and pulled out the canteen, opened it, and handed it around. Every one of the surviving First Squad took two shots. They had survived. However, the figures that came back caused one more round to go around. The first out of relief, but the second was for mourning of the 849 soldiers to go out to Site Indigo, there would be 225 casualties, three of which were from the 514 company. That would include CPL Pag, XO Lt. Adrian, and Captain Timothy, the company commander. After those had fallen, command of the 514 fell to Lt. Perry. Not one vehicle or radio was left intact after that night.

CHAPTER NINE

A Half-Day to Recover

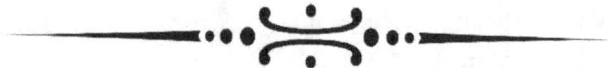

"We learn from failure, not from success!"

— Bram Stoker, *Dracula*

Lt. Colonel Swarts had a headache. His back was bruised, his shoulder blade felt funny, but he stood at the head of his table, the XO on his right, the CSM on is left. Before him, his company commanders and first sergeants of his companies, the 514, 514, 515, 517, 516, and 518; or what was left of the command teams. The 515, 513, and the 517 were the only intact command teams. The rest had to field promote whatever Lieutenant or Sergeant survived the massacre.

Two hundred and twenty-five casualties so far, and by all reports, no trucks were intact. They had no communication. The last time they reported in with the 549 Staff Duty was over five hours ago. It would be at least another twelve before the base would be concerned. Worse still, the ammo truck, slotted to arrive at 0300 hadn't come yet, and they had no way to raise them. Swarts was worried and he couldn't show it. His men needed him to be strong.

"Okay," said Swarts, "this was supposed to be a training mission, now it's become a fight for our lives. First question, did anyone bring a cellphone?"

The fourteen company Commanders and First Sergeants, as a collective gave the answer he didn't want to hear: that answer was no.

Swarts rolled his eyes. "Goddamn it! The one time they fully obey my order, this shit happens."

There were nervous chuckles but not much else, and that scared Swarts. Most of these men were combat veterans, battle hardened, it took a lot to shake them. They'd seen men blow up, evaporated, gunned down, and torn apart, but nothing like this. Forty unarmed combatants, with seemly super speed and strength, able to bend metal and send soldiers flying. This was something they weren't ready for. Never had they faced an enemy that wouldn't go down with a few bullets shot into them.

"Okay, suggestions?" Swarts questioned.

First Sergeant Hicks of the 515, the company that took half the casualties, said, "We should go, sir. Get to the nearest town, ring for help, and get MPs or Infantry from Fort Drum to secure the sight."

Swarts looked at FSG Hicks, his lips tight and said, "You're suggesting we abandon our equipment?"

"Yes, sir," said Hicks. "It's not worth lives, sir, lives that might be lost if we stay."

"We can't just abandon our equipment," said Captain Jones of the 513, a large black man who looked like hell, he himself having been slashed by one of those creatures in the face, using toilet paper to stop the flow of blood from the cuts he received from last night's attack. "There is millions of dollars' worth of it."

"Ain't worth shit compared to lives," snapped 2Lt. Redfur, the 518 only surviving officer, joined by SSG Iglesias, the highest surviving NCO.

"Don't you talk to me like that, boy," snapped Jones,

standing up so fast he knocked over a couple of paper coffee mugs, with Redfur, a whole foot and a half shorter, and less muscled also stood, glaring daggers at the captain. Swarts watched for a moment as they descended into fear. He knew it was fear. He knew fear that eroded a man's will, this was an example of it when you faced an unknown enemy. *Fear destroys a unit from the inside out*, his father once said, a veteran himself from Vietnam. Swarts had seen men succumb to fear more than once in the hell scape of a war.

Before he or his command team could stand and quiet them, another, louder voice said, "Gentlemen, please."

They quieted as a man entered the ECP. It was Captain Wright, the Battalion Chaplin. He was a large, beefy man of 40 with no hair and a heart of gold. He got lucky last night. The blood on his hands was not from his body but from the dead and wounded he tried to help. Unlike the others, he had a symbol of the cross sowed into his shoulder of his uniform, he had looks of daggers in his eyes. As the man of God for the battalion and the only man in the unit to not have a weapon, it was amazing how much he looked like he was about to rip some heads off.

"We have more dead boys and girls then wounded out there, and everyone out there is scared as hell. Six hundred twenty-four survived and wondering why we are at that number. This was supposed to be a field exercise. Now it a warzone, so whether we stay or go, it doesn't matter. We need to keep cool heads and come up with a plan to help us survive, that's it."

Lt. Colonel Swarts then stood, and said, "Thank you, Chaplin Wright." The Chaplin nodded and joined them at his place at the table. Swarts continued. "We have no communication, no working vehicles, so the only way to get out of here is to march. Okay, so, where do we go? The nearest town is over 30 miles from here. Could we make it before nightfall and get help? I don't know. What about our dead men and women out there? Do we leave them? And what if those things follow us? We could put civilians at risk. We can't do that either. So, what are our options?"

Major Dong spoke, "The ammo truck."

"It still hasn't come," said CSM Dickerson, her left eye puffy with bruises, her cheek cracked under her skin, making her barely move her mouth. "Probably got hit last night, too, for all we know."

"Yeah, but it might still be out there," said Major Dong, looking at the others. "We could rearm, and if the truck is intact, we could use it to get help."

"That's a lot of ifs," pointed out Captain Jones, dabbing at his face with cotton. "Plus, I can tell you from last night, bullets just pissed them off, and I doubt we have half of what we did have last night in terms of ammo. I don't know how we can kill these things."

Lt. Perry then spoke up, the only officer not to do so thus far. First Sergeant Michael looking down at the table; he having a slashed shoulder from last night.

"One of my soldiers managed to kill one," he said quietly.

They all looked at him with looks of disbelief and surprise on their faces.

"How?" asked 2Lt. Redfur, trying not to sound jealous.

"She managed to stab it with a tent stake. It drove right through its heart."

He went into his tale. He described the events that lead to the death of the creature that attacked Jenny last night. When finished, Lt. Perry then recounted how he was helping to get the injured to the medics. They were already overworked, this forced soldiers with combat lifesaving certifications to join them and treat the injured. Five medics were also among the dead, and the dead were quickly piling up. He went back to 514 base camp and saw one SPC Jenny staring at one of the bodies. He was about to scold her until he noticed that it was wearing civilian pants and a hoodie. At this distance it looked like a teenager, with a long wooden tent stake impaled into its chest. He walked to Jenny, who, upon seeing him, stood at attention.

"At ease," said Lt. Perry, "relax."

"Yes, sir," said Jenny, turning back to the body, shining her red tinted flashlight on it. Lt Perry was briefed on what Jenny did to this thing a few hours ago. She got lucky in killing it, but it was all good, now they had a body of one of the creatures to study. That was when Perry looked down and his heart skipped a beat. The creature was paler than bone, its flesh glowing eerily in the red light. Its ears were pointed; its black eyes open, staring at the sky, its mouth open with black blood trickling from it. Then he saw the veins. They weren't there before, showing blackly in the setting moon and the slowly rising sun, seeming to blacken as the sun rose higher.

"It's changing," said Jenny, "those veins weren't there before."

Lt Perry looked at it, noticing its skin seemed to be turning a black shade of narcosis, its once sharp teeth seemed to be in an extreme rate of decay. The first rays of the rising sun finally rose behind the two, soldiers milling, helping their wounded comrades, or trying to do what they could to repair their damaged equipment, without much success. Then, the decaying body started to smoke. It wasn't noticeable at first, but then Perry saw the first traces coming from the body, the smoke trailing up to the sky in a thin stream from its mouth. Then more came and it waffled out like a chimney.

"What the hell?" asked Jenny, as the smoke became fire.

"Dang, get back!"

Perry grabbed Jenny, dragging her back away from the burning corpse, its chest bursting into flames, its legs and arms soon followed. Perry looked at the rising sun, then back at the corpse, its body engulfed, then it crumbled in on itself, the flaming flesh becoming ash, and it soon died out, the body having burned away, only leaving ash, blackened grass behind.

"Oh my god," said Jenny.

The end of Lt. Perry's tale came with complete quiet from the room, even Cpt. Jones didn't notice the blood dripping from his makeshift bandage and hitting the cuff of his uniform. Then First Sergeant Hicks spoke.

"Are we fighting fucking vampires now? Seriously, I want to know."

Captain Wright spoke up, "Don't matter what they are. We now know we can kill them."

"With stakes," muttered 2Lt. Redburn, fear, and contempt in his eyes, "this is some bullshit."

Colonel Swarts spoke, "Lt. Perry, your company has all the mechanics; can we get some vehicles up in time?"

Perry looked at FSG Michael for a moment, who shook his head.

"No, sir, I don't think we can, not before tonight, and I bet you anything they will come back tonight."

Swarts nodded, and asked, "Your unit had three causalities, right?"

"Yes, sir."

Swarts stood and said, "The rest of you, I want the camp's defenses made tighter. Hell, bring in the C-Wire if you have too.

I want to make it as hard as hell for these things to reach us. Give ammo only to the best shooters in your squad, those who shoot at minimum 35 out of 40 during the range."

Then First Sergeant Diosa, the only other female NCO inside beside the CSM, spoke up. "Are we all forgetting something? We haven't been in contact with Fort Drum in hours. We are supposed to contact Staff Duty every hour. We are five hours late. Surely they will send help."

They all looked at the command team and Major Dong spoke. "They will not send anyone out for at least 36 hours. This was supposed to be a training mission."

The collective *the fuck* almost broke the group again.

Swarts yelled, "Silence! We don't know that. They could send someone sooner. But we just have to last one more night, okay. Now, go with my instructions. Let's try not to lose any more men tonight."

They all grumbled their submissions.

Captain Jones added, "We should also bring out as many axes and pickaxes as we have. We know tent stakes work. Maybe metal will work better."

"Good call," said Swarts. "Now, Chaplin, continue helping the wounded and do what you can to help our soldiers. The rest of you, except for 514, start preparing for defense. Lt. Perry, FSG Michael, stay for a moment. Everyone else, dismissed."

They got up, only Lt. Perry and FSG Michael staying with the Colonel. He gave them a look and Perry noticed it denoted sadness.

"I need your company to do something and you're not going to like it. This will be enacted if you can't get any of the vehicles up before sundown, understood."

They both nodded. Swarts gave them their instructions. He

was right, they didn't like it.

***

"Fuck," growled Hickman, moving away from his LMTV. It was just trashed. The fuel tank and air collectors were on the ground, the tires slashed, oil leaking everywhere, and the radiator was punched through. Coolant and oil were mixing. And this was the upped-armored one, and it was one of the few that were relatively intact.

Jenny crawled out of the bottom of another vehicle, this one a HMMV, stood, her coveralls smeared with oil.

"Anything?" she asked.

"Nah, this one is trashed, too," he said, his cheek and eye puffy with bruising. The skin was dark purple.

"We can't get any of these vehicles repaired without a motorpool," said Jenny.

"And to get them to the motorpool, we need to repair them." said Hickman, in an almost sing song voice. "What an interesting conundrum."

Jenny held back a chuckle, and went to the rear of the vehicle, and when she cleared the back end looked over to the place where that, that thing nearly got her. She remembered the teeth, so close, those black eyes; eyes that reminded her of Madam Roseta story.

No, she thought. *Don't you think it. That wasn't a vampire. Those are things of myth, even Madam Roseta didn't believe…;* but she had believed. At one point during her life, she had feared the thing from her father's story. She had believed, maybe not consciously, but she had believed. The black eyes, the sharp teeth, the pointed ears; could it be?

"Stop it," she hissed, "stop."

"I'm not doing anything," said Hickman, looking over, confused.

Jenny looked up; realizing Hickman was still in the area, overhearing her whispering to herself.

"Sorry, just thinking about that... that thing."

Hickman looked over, grimacing, remembering how that thing batted him aside like a toddler.

"Jenny," he began, "you think they will be coming back again tonight?"

"I don't know."

Then Sergeant Garcia came up.

"Any luck?"

"Well, we could fix this one, Sergeant," said Hickman, jabbing a finger behind him at the same truck he had looked over, at the same moment, the driver side mirror fell off behind them. "All we need is a professional garage and a new truck."

She looked at the cab, noticing deep gouges in the armor of the truck, those made by claw marks.

"How the fuck did they do that?" muttered Garcia, crossing herself.

Jenny shrugged, "Don't know."

"So, you got no way to fix her up?"

"Could try calling AAA," said Hickman, then snorted. "Oh, wait, we can't."

"Well, come with me, don't worry about changing out, the Lieutenant, I mean the new commander wants to see his troops in a formation."

They both nodded, both knowing they weren't getting anywhere. They followed Sergeant Garcia, who was leading them to what was guard point two.

"Any luck," asked Jenny, "with any other truck?"

"No," she said, "they were fast and too thorough. Those motherfuckers slashed everything that would cripple it; then moved on. The radios didn't fare much better. They even got the ones inside the trucks, everyone those from the ECP Forward or the guard posts."

Hickman looked back at the truck. "That explains the driver side doors."

"Think we can fix any of them?" asked Jenny.

"Nope," she said, pointing to a HMMV whose engine was revealed, the hood having been torn from its body, revealing an engine and a slashed up inside, reminding Jenny of a deer she had found on the side of the road, its lower half missing its insides, organs and bones beneath the flesh. She shivered, not wanting to think what that thing would have done to her if she didn't have the tent stake in hand. That three foot long, busted piece of wood had saved her life. They reached where the assembled soldiers were, all 139, no, 136 of them. They stood there, tired, some bruised, others not injured. They found Hamish, who fell in with them. Lt. Perry stood there, the other two surviving Lieutenants, Lt. Rima and Lt. Silverheels, along with the company First Sergeant, stood with him, none looking too happy.

"Everyone here?" asked Lt. Perry over the din. After it was confirmed by the Platoon Sergeants, the Lieutenant spoke.

"Want the truth; can we get any of these vehicles running in the next twelve hours?"

All the 91 bravos and everyone else who worked on mechanics shook their heads.

"No, sir," said SFC Cruise, of Second Platoon. "Not without a motorpool."

"Radios?" he asked.

SFC Tull spoke up, "We found a couple just slashed and my guys are trying to cobble something together."

"How many can you realistically get up?"

Tull shook his head, "One, sir, maybe, and that is a big maybe."

"How many men do you need?"

Tull thought it over. "Two, three at most."

"Pick them now," said Perry, First Sergeant, cross armed, standing next to him, his oriental features twisted up in a deep frown, looking down at the ground.

SFC Tull, who was a large black man with a shaven head, and a tough looking face, looked at Lt. Perry in surprise. But he obeyed. He turned his head and said, "Deraps, Gentry, go to the Lieutenant."

SPC Deraps, a blonde man from Texas, and PFC Gentry, a brown haired, pimply boy from Boston, ran forward, the Lieutenant whispering instructions to them when he got there. Jenny, like the others, strained to hear, but failed. A minute later, the two ran off, heading for the ECP.

Perry turned to the others and said, "Men, we have a mission, and I have no idea how dangerous it is. The Colonel has asked our company to take this risk, but I won't ask any of you to go unless you volunteer. I know I'm not the XO or the Commander, but now I hold the position. Few of you know me. But now, I'm going to ask all of you to trust me."

Nobody said a word, waiting for what was to come.

"The Battalion Commander recognizes we are in a bad position. No vehicle is intact, and all of our radios are pretty much toast. He believes we will get help, at best, in 36 hours. After the attack last night by those vam... by those creatures, we don't know if we have that kind of time. Thanks to SPC Jenny, we know they can be killed."

At this, just for a second, all eyes were on Jenny, who blushed and looked away. She still felt like she was getting too much credit. It had only been an accident that she managed to kill it. What she didn't know, that while all eyes were on her, Hamish and Sergeant Garcia squeezed hands for a moment in marital comfort.

"Because of this, the 514 has been strongly requested to undertake a mission. Our mission is to go to the nearest town where we can call up Fort Drum and get help. Our secondary objective is to find the ammo truck if we can, have them call up Fort Drum, and get them to get the ammo to the field. Once we tell them were to go, we are to continue to the town, stay put, and get evac from there."

There was a murmur of interest, and even Jenny felt a faint tinge of hope. How far could the nearest town be?

"The nearest town is more than 70 miles away. It's called Malone, New York."

There was silent, but obvious *oh fuck* looks on all the soldier's faces, and under his breath, only caught by Jenny was said by Hickman, "Oh, shit."

"Seventy miles!" yelled a Dominican Sergeant named Sergeant Sanchez. "And if those things find us out there, we'll be slaughtered."

"We believe we will be safe, at least during the daytime," explained Perry.

"Then why not just send a few!" yelled SSG Lee, Platoon Sergeant of Second Platoon. "Make them less noticeable."

"Give it more of a fighting chance to reach Malone," said Perry. "If they find us gone, we don't think all of them will hunt us at once. That might give us an edge. If only a few go and those things find out, we know one of us can't fight them alone. But I leave it up to you. If only I and a few others to go, so be it, but, if we all go, we might stand a better chance."

A buzzing happened, and Jenny saw that things were falling apart. She knew what she had to do. Ever since it was realized by the company that she killed one of these things, she had people come to her, asking how she survived. She tried to avoid being the hero of the company because she didn't think she deserved it. It didn't save CPL Pag. But now, she knew she had to be that person, and she stepped forward, and seeing her, the 134 soldiers went quiet as she stood among them. She gulped, and looked over at Sergeant Garcia and SFC Alibudbun, who both nodded encouragement to her.

"Last night, we lost over 200 men and women, at home, on our turf. We got lucky they left when they did. I was almost killed by one of those things. I'm not hurt, but it would have killed me. I got lucky and it ran into a tent stake I was holding. I was lucky. But now we know we can kill these things. And we can find other ways. I stabbed it through the heart, and it died in seconds. And we have other weapons. If a stake can kill them, why not an axe; a pickaxe; or a sledgehammer? I don't know why they could almost shrug off live rounds, but they do hurt them a bit. If we stay, we might find another way to kill them, and there is safety in numbers. But if we go, we have a chance to get help sooner, and save more of our battle buddies. I don't want to go out there anymore than you do, but I will go with Lt. Perry alone if I have to. But if we all go, we might have a chance."

There were new murmurs, murmurs of interest. Perry stepped forward. "I can't tell you that you are going to be alright. That would be a lie. But there's a chance. If we take it, we could save more lives. We have all rucked 30 miles at least once during out career, and we can do 70 no problem. We won't get there tonight, but we might make it there the next day. If we manage this, we can get everyone else evacuated."

"Why wouldn't we get there today?" asked SSG Lee. "Seventy miles is a long walk, but it..."

"We are not taking the roads," explained Perry, "we are going through the woods to make it harder for us to find."

"Mofo's crazy," muttered Hickman to Hamish, who grinned back.

"So, who is willing to go?"

For a moment, no one raised their hand, but after a moment, Jenny did. She was the first. Then, good old Amish boy Hamish did as well. As did Hickman, Jackson, Sosa, Sergeant Sengel, and Sergeant Garcia. Good old First Squad of Third Platoon, always the first to raise their hands. Then SFC Alibudbun and the rest of Third Platoon. Then Second, then Fourth, then finally First Platoon.

Perry nodded, and said, "Get whatever stakes, axes, and pickaxes we have. All live ammo will go to those who scored 35 out of 40 in the platoon. Everyone else will use the hand weapons. Rucks have MREs, one day's change of clothing, E-tool, and medical kits for the Combat Lifesavers. We leave in two hours. Uniform, OCPs, IOTVs, and Kevlars will stay put. They didn't work well last night, might as well not wear anything that would slow us down. Move out."

They did, Jenny hoping that she hadn't convinced her battles to sign a death warrant.

CHAPTER TEN

12 Hours Earlier

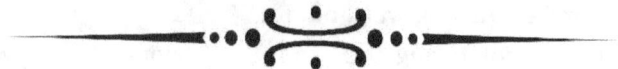

"Terror, on its surface, cuts hard and sharp as a knife, but at its heart, it swells and rolls like a sea. It isn't fixed into permanent shapes or symbols or even shadows. It's liquid, and we ingest it, and it ingests us."

— John Marks, *Fangland*

SSG Warren, assigned to the rear guard because of his bad leg, waited at the radio for the call to come in at Staff Duty. He was worried. He had been worried for the past three hours. His concern started nine hours ago. He wasn't a man who overly concerned himself in the military. Most of the training protocols were bull. And taking soldiers cellphones away during a training mission, fuck, what was the brass thinking? Now, he and his Staff Duty runner, a blonde kid, SPC Parker, had spent every hour checking the radio. The field was considered active at 1300. The first reports came in at 1500, with the CPT calling into the radio stationed in Staff Duty, recorded on the staff duty log, and every hour they sent up reports, recorded by Staff Duty.

It was at 2000 when the problem came, after his checks. The last report was sent up at that time, recorded by his Staff Duty Runner at 2005. When he settled back in at 2059, Parker told him he was going to take a dump real fast. He took off running down the hall. The moment SSG Warren heard the bathroom door shut, it was 2100 hours. They hadn't called yet, but Site Indigo should soon. At 2103, still nothing. Then 2106, nothing, and Parker came back and took over radio again. Next, 2119; okay this was getting concerning.

At 2140, SPC Parks tried calling them up.

"ECP Forward, this is 549 SBSD, do you read?"

Nothing. He tried again, still nothing. He then tried calling up the ammo truck's radio, but SSG Warren pointed out that unlike the one they used at the field, that one by now would be out of range.

At 2300, and putting in his log, 'No contact with ECP, forward 2100 or 2200', he picked up the Staff Duty phone and dialed up Lt. Miranda, the OIC in charge of Staff Duty. She picked up on the first ring.

"Hello," said a female voice.

"Ma'am, sorry to disturb you, this SSG Warren who is on Staff Duty. I need to report the ECP Forward hasn't reported up for the past two hours."

Silence for a moment then, "I don't think this is cause for alarm SSG. Maybe their having radio trouble."

"Yes ma'am. However, the radio they are using is connected to a transceiver that reaches Fort Drum, like the one we have here at Staff Duty. However, the radio itself is a standard model and can be swapped out with any other radio."

"What about the receiver?"

"They have two spares ma'am, but again, it doesn't add up to me."

A moment of silence. "Okay, I'll be in their at 0200. If they haven't brought back communications by then, we will make some calls."

"Yes ma'am."

He hung up, Parks still trying to reach ECP Forward.

The time pasted, and at 0150, he recalled Lt. Miranda, who confirmed she was coming, and then waited. Ten minutes later, 549 front door opened, and a beautiful black woman with braided hair, and an Arab man in civilian clothing came behind her, S3 Sergeant Major Curry.

"Attention!" yelled Warren, going to his feet. While he respected Curry more, Lt. Miranda was an officer, and her rank was higher than his, though he had vaster experience.

"Carry on," said Miranda, and she and Curry entered the Staff Duty office, Parks still on the radio.

"Still no word?" asked SGM Curry.

"No, Sergeant Major."

"Did you check the receiver on our end?"

SSG Warren blushed. "No, Sergeant Major, I uhhhh, I hadn't."

"Easy mistake to make," said Curry, showing he was not angry, beating the Lieutenant, who looked like she was going to chew him out. He turned to SPC Parks and asked, "You a radio man, son?"

"No, Sergeant Major."

"Come with me, I used to work on radios back in my day. We'll figure it out. Lieutenant, could you operate the radio while we are out there? Have to run some tests."

She nodded as the two left, calling into the radio. After an hour they came back, and SGM Curry said, "Well, our radio is working fine."

SSG Warren was relieved. But it soon gave way to concern.

"So, why can't they reach us?"

"Don't know. Let's wait until 0500. Specialist, can you put coffee on? I have a pot in my office."

He tossed Parks the key to his office and he took off.

As they waited, drank coffee, and shooting the shits, it helped relax the group. Then 0500 came up. Nothing.

"Okay," said Lt. Miranda, "I'm going to call Captain Choi, the rear guard OIC."

"Smart," said Curry, who now looked a little concerned. "See if he can contact the Brigade Commander as well."

She nodded and made the call. Colonel Norris was in her office at 0600, getting some work in when her phone rang.

"Colonel Norris speaking."

"Ma'am, this is Captain Choi. I feel obligated to tell you that our field mission camp has not reported in for almost ten hours. We are preparing to send some people out within two hours in an TMP and see what is going on."

"Everything okay?"

"We are not sure ma'am."

"Okay, do so, and thank you for informing me. I'll inform General Bryant. He seemed to take a special interest in this mission."

"Yes ma'am."

She hung up and called General Bryant's cellphone.

"General Bryant speaking."

"General, I thought you should know that the 549 field mission has lost the ability to communicate."

A moment of silence. "Are you certain?"

"Yes, sir, I have been informed by Captain Choi of the 549's rear guard that their sending an TMP out to investigate and..."

"Negative," said General Bryant.

For a moment, Colonel Norris was too stunned to speak,

then, "Sir, I..."

"This field mission was supposed to be as real as possible. We can't jump the gun only because they could be having minor radio problems. Instruct Captain Choi to wait another 24 hours."

"Twenty-four hours?" Norris had to control her voice, her brown hair thrown forward, "Sir, with all due respect, the maximum is 36 hours."

"Twenty-four, that is an order!" snapped Bryant. "Send it now."

He hung up, and Colonel Norris starred at the phone, shocked by what just happened. What the fuck was going on here? This was not like the General.

Controlling the urge to disobey, she called back Captain Choi, who, after a moment of arguing, obeyed, and hung up. Guilt filled her heart, but she had to just hope that this wasn't a colossal mistake.

CHAPTER ELEVEN

And the Night Came

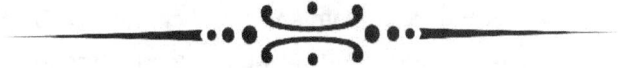

"for in the absence of God he had found Man. Man killing man, man helping man, both of them anonymous: the scourge and the blessing."

— Guillermo del Toro and Chuck Hogan, *The Strain*

Hickman was smoking a cigarette as they marched. All 134 members of the 514 SMC went along in two columns. They marched in silence. They weren't wearing IOTVs or Kevlars, and not all were carrying rifles. Only about forty of them were, which included Hickman, having scored a forty out of forty at the last range. Jenny and Hamish, having scored only 28 and 32 respectively, were given axes. They were two of the lucky ones. The company only had twenty axes and ten pickaxes with them. They were doled out to the first soldiers in line. The rest got tent stakes, two each, 5-50 cord tied around them, and slung on their backs under their assault packs.

They marched fast, and slow at the same time. Fast was the pace, slow because of the forest march, lack of cellphone GPS's, and they were forced to use a map to find Malone. Sergeant Ceno, a hunched, bespectacled NCO of Third Platoon had a map of the area with them. He was forced on consult every twenty minutes or so. They left the field at 0935. It was now 1300, and they had only covered 7 miles.

Four steps later, Lt. Perry ordered a halt to the march, again, for the sixteenth time, and he and First Sergeant joined Sergeant Ceno.

Jenny sat down with Hamish and Hickman, who was still smoking a cigarette, the menthol Kool trailing smoke into the skies. They were in woods, working their way to the main road, hoping to find a civilian vehicle they could flag down. They were still a long way off though, and the protection of the sun slowly trickled away, the sky seeming to become dimmer with each passing hour.

"Man," said Hickman, drinking out of his hydration kit, "thought it would be easier. With all the PT we do back home, thought marching like this would be a breeze."

"Forgot how time slows down when you march," muttered Hamish, also drinking.

"At least the sun is still up," said Jenny, thankful it wasn't a cloudy day.

"Yeah," said Hickman, "for what, six, seven more hours?"

Sergeant Garcia walked up with Sergeant Sengel. They both looked down at the sweating, tired soldiers.

"You guys okay?" asked Sergeant Garcia, trying not to make eye contact with Hamish.

"We are okay," said Hickman, still smoking, less than a quarter cigarette left, "just getting sick of these stops."

"Map reading is slow," said Sergeant Sengel, his Togolese tones belaying tiredness, "we will get there."

"We will stop for a few at 1900," said Sergeant Garcia, "Then we'll get some rest, hopefully somewhere defendable. Then we will keep moving."

"Wow," murmured Hickman, "at this rate, by 1900 we might

actually cover another mi..."

"Hickman," snapped Garcia, "I'll smoke you if you finish that sentence."

Hickman was about to snap back, when he stopped, looked up, took a breath, and said, "Yes, Sergeant."

Garcia nodded. Despite the fact he knew about her marriage to Hamish, Hickman wouldn't betray them by snapping off at her. It would harm her, her marriage, and the squad. As the two NCOS walked off, Hickman said, "Man, this is hard."

Jackson and Sosa came up. Sosa said, "You guys doing good?"

"Yeah," said Jenny, "we are fine."

Jackson plunked his large ass down and said, "So, think we have any vampires coming tonight?"

The other four started.

"Vampires? Don't..." began Hamish but was interrupted by Jackson.

"Come on, fangs, supernatural speed and strength, only killed with a stake through the heart, that screams vampire."

The others were silent, trying not to think what they were almost ready to admit. They couldn't admit it. Jenny knew this, because she tried to deny it, even when she watched that thing burn in the sun, after she stabbed it in the heart. Could it... no, no, there had to be some other explanation. Vampires weren't real, they weren't!

"Let's go!" yelled Lt. Perry. Jenny relieved, stood, trying not to think of Roseta's story.

***

Lt. Colonel Swarts stood in the field, watching his men finish the defenses for the nights possible on coming attack. The C-

Wire was brought in to defend the 490 remaining soldiers after the 514 left, and they were working hard, preparing for the night.

The camp, that had been widespread earlier, was now condensed. Some of the tents were moved closer together, other were just taken down to make room, the stakes used as weapons now. The C-Wire had been brought in, only about hundred feet away from the outskirts of the reorganized camp. Behind this sharp circle was a field of upside down tent poles, their butts buried into the dirt, their tips sticking out of the ground. About five hundred were spread out in a second circle behind the tent. Behind that, 90 men and women with rifles sat in makeshift shelters or quickly dug fox holes. Armed with M4's and 249 SAW guns, they had enough ammo to last the night, they hoped. Behind them, men and women who were armed with axes, pickaxes, remaining tent poles, knives, and whatever else they could get. This included one man who was armed with a makeshift spear, made out of copper grounding rods and a Gerber taped to the top of the staff with duct tape.

Colonel Swarts looked out with his command team, Major Dong and Sergeant Major Dickerson observing their defenses, knowing it wouldn't be enough, the broken metal and rubber from the vehicles and radios on the ground before them attesting to that fact. He saw a few men smoking in the fox holes, and while normally they would be yelled at by now, this time they were given a pass. They were scared, and Lt. Colonel Swarts figured the smoke would keep them a little calmer, so he let them have it.

He looked up; 1700 hours, the night was on its way, and he prayed to survive this second night. He also prayed the 514 were going to get their butts in gear and get help soon.

Orson looked down at the camp three hours later, licking his lips, looking down at the assembled defenses before them. The human's camp had been condensed, and he saw a picket line made of C-Wire, wooden stakes before the four large tents, and several foxholes. The others were with him as well; the smell of dirt was strong. They had slept in the ground about twelve miles south of the camp. Using the dirt they brought with them from their coffins, they sprinkled it on the ground and were able to sleep, no trouble.

"Makes it more fun," he said, a small grin on his face, Lee-Arne and Legwang looking down at him. Lee-Arne was smiling, Legwang looked bored.

"Their adapting," said Legwang.

"Just makes it more exciting," growled Lee-Arne. There was a collective growl from the others assembled around them.

"Yes, and do you not notice there seems to be fewer of them than what we left alive from last night?" muttered Legwang, pointing at the camp.

"Probably more died from injuries," snarled Orson.

"Or," said Wegwong, smiling slightly, as his ivory skin glowed in the darkness, "a few of them left."

"Why would they do that?" asked Lee-Arne, "Abandon their comrades?"

"Isn't it odd, you think we'd be alone in this world here, in this place," said Wegwong with a grin, his boyish face looking even younger. "And yet, nearby, there are whole towns within reach. Strange isn't it, that of the illusion of distance?"

"What are you talking about, old man?" snapped Orson.

"We were asleep for twelve hours. Is it not possible that, say, a group of a hundred or so might have had the idea to try and get some help, and wouldn't they have over twelve hours to reach a town nearby to get help, and maybe arrive tonight or tomorrow."

Orson looked down at the camp, a look of concern on his face. It was possible, but... no, they wouldn't... would they?

He turned to two ivory vampires, who he nicknamed Cheech and Chong, the two having very dark senses of humor. One was originally a Ku Klux Klan member from Alabama, the other a former Mongolian Hun.

"Go find the missing ones," he said, simply, "and kill them all."

The two nodded and took off, their bodies blurring as they ran.

Their numbers, now 37, he turned to his remaining vampires and said, "Go; and nobody get staked tonight please, that was embarrassing. Take your fill, but feel free to play with your food."

***

A scream broke the silence of the night, a loud, animalistic scream that the soldiers knew, that SSG Gear remembered from last night, getting a slashed, and now bandaged, shoulder from the perpetrators of that scream. He saw the ivory and obsidian creatures coming out of the woods, their bodies glowing in the bright moon light.

"Here they come!" yelled the SSG Gear, commanding the forward defenses, rifles raised, the ones without guns looking nervous.

The creatures started flying down the hill, going fast, claws out to the sides, fangs bare, and their mouths wider than they should have been.

"Open fire!" yelled Gear, in range of four guard post. Bullets flew from ten guns, hitting a row of a dozen vampires in the chest. They fell to the ground as the others ran past.

A cheer that came from the soldiers died when those same creatures that fell stood back up after a moment and started running again. Gear's mouth opened in fear for a moment, then closed it; five tours in Afghanistan and Iraq teaching him not to show fear.

"Fire again!" he yelled.

Again, bullets flew, and again, the much closer creature fell, about six, but they stood up again. They were less than seventy feet away when Gear ordered the third volley. This time, sixteen fell, but again they stood, small amount of black blood appearing on their clothing, but were running again within moments. They reached the C-wire then leaped. They landed gracefully, avoiding the stakes. More and more leapt, and ran to the camp, hitting the guard post and hitting them hard, but when the last one leapt, SSG Gear raised his rifle, it slowly falling to the ground, its ivory body shimmering in the moon light. Following it down, Gear fired a shot, aided by his ACOG, hitting the creature full in the face. As it fell, Gear swore he saw the things face healing, that was, until it hit the stake, its wooden frame breaking through its body and penetrated its heart. A death cry of a Tasmanian devil and a demon came flying out into the night, the creature in its death throws, trying to free itself, but dying all the same.

Gear was about to cry in relief, that was until a female version of one of those things appeared in front of him. He tried to raise his rifle, but he heard a sick snap from his arms, the creature breaking them with a fierce jerk as she took his rifle, his shoulders dislocated as well, and arms going to his side, useless as dead snakes hanging from a nail. Before he could scream in pain, the creature was upon him, knocking him back as her mouth full of fangs bit into his neck, draining him of his blood, sucking away the man's life force as well as the pain.

When Lt. Colonel Swarts saw this shot, he was about to cheer when one of the obsidian versions of the creatures, female looking, rushed forward, broke the Staff Sergeant's arms, and feed on him. Armed with an axe, and over the objections of his command team, he rushed forward in a vein hope to save him. He ran, and then felt his feet leave the ground. He flew, head over heels, desperately holding the axe, trying to land in a way where injury was avoidable. He landed on his back, the creature running forward, fangs exposed, shockingly white to the pure black of the creature's flesh.

Swarts raised his arms in desperation but instead of fangs, he heard a wet hacking sound above him. A second one came and there was a thud to the left of him, and he felt something heave and land on his chest, something wet dripping onto his neck, and the smell of copper in the air. He opened his eyes. Black blood was dripping on to his chest from the thing on top of him, a headless corps of the creature that attacked him. He pushed it off him and stood, seeing CSM Dickerson above him, axe in her hands.

"Sir," she said around her still broken jaw, and helped Swarts up, surprising strength in her arms.

"Damn!" he said, looking back at the headless corpse. "You got it."

The pointed eared bastard was still nearby, its mouth still open ready to bite. Ignoring this, Swarts looked around at the carnage. The creatures leapt on to his men like animals in the hunt, biting their necks. A few soldiers tried to take advantage of this to shoot at the thing to take it down, but it did not seem to work, even as bullets pierced their sides, and seemingly healing over in seconds. The creatures would stand when they were done and more usually then not just mow through these soldiers in seconds, the claws taking chunks and limbs from the soldiers.

"Come on!" he yelled, the Command Sergeant Major followed, axes in hand. They ducked and dodged bodies and body parts thrown around them like confetti, droplets of blood peppering them, as screams hit their ears.

He saw twenty soldiers fighting one of the ivory versions of the creatures, shooting at it, but it dodged and rushed them, sending four flying and slashing at four others with her claws, blood spurting from their arteries, the creature opening its mouth, trying to catch some of it.

"Come..." began Swarts but heard a scream. He turned to his Sergeant Major, seeing one of the creatures, another ivory one was on her, its teeth at her neck, her body decompressing from the blood loss like a juice box being sucked to the last drop.

"No!" he yelled rushing back and raising the axe, bringing it down on the feeding creature's neck. Blade hit flesh, then bone, then went out the other side, the axe breaking the CSM's neck bones, killing her. He kicked at the headless creature, putting it on its back, black blood still spurting from its neck. He brought the axe down in a futile attempt at revenge, hitting it with the axe in the chest, only stopping when a scream came out. The combat paused, all the creatures looking up, and screamed in kind. Then they turned and ran: the 34 survivors. Of the soldiers, only 139 remained. Once they were counted, LTC Swarts knew they would not survive another night. Chaplin Wright started praying.

***

The 514 found a secured spot, dropped their packs, and got

ready for a quick rest. It was 1900 hours, and they were tired. Lt. Perry allotted four hours of sleep. Good news, no vampires, bad news, they got lost and, in the end, only covered 20 miles and added one extra mile to their trip.

Jenny put her pack with her squad, who lay on the ground, exhausted. Even Sergeant Garcia, the strongest and toughest of First Squad, Third Platoon, looked tired. She sat next to Hamish, the closest they'd been in hours. Sengel looked at them all, yawning, and said, "No guard duty tonight, Second and Forth has it."

"Thank god," moaned Hickman, dropping where he was and closing his eyes, "I swear if we get out of this, I'll take that trip to see my mother."

Jenny chuckled, "How about a week with no booze?"

"Twenty bucks says I can do it."

"I'll take that bet," said Hamish, smiling.

Garcia chuckled and said, "Get some sleep; we will be there tomorrow, hopefully."

They all lay down and closed their eyes.

Sergeant Miller of Second Squad, Third Platoon, watched over his 134 charges with six other soldiers. He was on for three hours, and then would go to bed. He was partnered with SPC Willis tonight in the dark, cold night air. Willis was a white kid, big but not overly so, with brown hair and eyes. Miller was short, African American, and worried. The things hadn't arrived yet... those, fuck it, he'd admit it to himself... those vampires. He'd been calling them that when he saw one sucking CPL Peg dry during the first attack, and prayed they were going to be spared tonight.

Willis went for a cigarette, meaning to light it, but Miller smacked his hand.

"No smoke, not tonight, kid."

"Nothing is happening," moaned Willis, looking forlornly at the now dirt covered cig on the ground which was flicked further by Miller.

"That's what worries me."

Five minutes passed; then a half hour; then an hour. At an hour and a half, Miller started to relax and turn to Willis to tell him it was okay to smoke when a scream hit the air, so eerily like Tasmanian devils.

"Oh, shit!" yelled Willis as fire came from Forth Platoon's guard post, and Miller saw another ivory figure almost flying before them. He fired his rifle as the creature leapt forward, the bullets missing its legs, one clawed hand down, and it connected with Willis' head, taking it off with a sickening, wet, ripping sound, blood spurting from the neck.

Miller screamed, "We're under attack. Everyone take cover!"

The bullets awoke Jenny and the others who grabbed their weapons, but the creatures were in the sleeping crowd, slashing through them, being caught with their pants down. Jobe lost his life during this opening attack, the same flying creature that killed Willis punched him right through the gut, lifting him up, and biting down on his neck. The only mercy in this was Jobe didn't wake up. Jackson screamed upon seeing this as his friend was tossed away like a wet, overfilled garbage bag.

The second creature mowed half of Fourth Squad down, its claws ripping through them like switch blades.

Blood and bullets went flying in the confusion, a few dying of friendly fire as the vampires attacked, everyone trying to catch them but no managing to get them. A few flares were thrown to give the soldiers light, but a few had their NVG's on to see, and got blinded, one soldier so bad that he didn't notice that the flare landed on his back after he fell to all fours, clutching his head, the flare setting his clothing on fire until it was too late, the man ended up burning to death.

The First Sergeant went down, trying to tackle one, and getting ripped in half for his efforts. SFC Tull charged but was sent flying by the larger of the two creatures. Jenny was frozen in place alongside Hickman, separated from First Squad due the confusion, tried to find one of the things in the chaos. They did. It landed in front of them. It was as pale as the one Jenny killed, but he had a beer gut, a beard, and wore a blue wind breaker and slacks, blood covering its beard, a swastika tattooed on its neck. It smiled, and Hickman knowing what it was doing, its fangs glinting, grabbed Jenny and tackled her to the ground, the claw missing them by inches, praying in a vain hope, hearing the screams of the dying, that it would go away. It didn't; and prepared for another strike, smiling down at its victims.

"Hey!" yelled a voice, causing all three to look for its source. It was Garcia, she held a knife in her hand, raised it, and without hesitation, sliced her palm. The creature, seeing this, grinned even wider and started to her.

"No!" yelled Jenny standing but the creature batted her away and she was sent sprawling by its version of a light touch.

Hickman tried to grab its foot, but it shook him off as Garcia held out her knife, blade down, ready to fight for her soldiers. Hickman had no intentions of letting her die. He stood, and saw two rifle men trying to run, one small Asian girl and one tall Latino guy, and Hickman turned them around as the creature headed towards Garcia, her face set in stone.

"Shoot that mother!" he yelled at the other two, all three raising their rifles, and Garcia, seeing this, dropped. The creature, confused, paused at this development, and turned to Hickman. *Fuck*, thought Hickman, *it's a goddamned vampire* then raised his rifle as did the other two.

The vampire, as Hickman referred to him for the rest of his life, in confusion, saw the rifles, and ran, in a blur, to its right, just as they pulled their triggers. The first bullet missed it. The second made a slash in the rear of his pants. The third though, Hickman's bullet, managed to hit it where the leg met the hip. The creature tried to leap, but its own momentum sent it spinning. What Hickman and the others didn't know was that Hamish, who had heard his wife call, turned, and tried to save her, was charging with an axe, and seeing the creature in midair, raised it when he reached it and made a clean sweep through its neck, beheading it. Hamish screamed a scream of anger and destruction, wanting to destroy the monster.

Jenny got back to her feet, joined Hickman as they got to Hamish, his body tense, staring at the creature's head with pure rage and disgust on his face, it daring to hurt those who he cared about, and made it pay the ultimate price.

Jenny went to him, he still standing there, and she put a hand on him. "Hamish," she said gently, and he seemed to come back to life.

Hickman rushed forward and slapped his shoulder. "Got that mofo."

Then Garcia came forward, throwing her arms around Hamish, dropping her own knife.

"What were you thinking?" cried Hamish, holding her with one arm, the other still holding his axe.

"Saving my dumbass soldier," she sobbed back, her face in his chest.

Jenny and Hickman stood awkwardly for a moment until the

screams hit them again. They forgot there was still one more vampire. They rushed forward and the second smaller creature mowing through two squads of soldiers. More blood was flowing, spraying from the soldiers like sprinklers from their necks. Three charged in, tent stakes held like clubs. It took them down in four seconds.

Jenny felt her foot lightly hit something on the ground as she ran and looked down. A dud flare was on the ground. No, not a dud, it hadn't been lit. She looked up at the rampaging creature, its ivory skin now drenched in blood. She saw its black eyes. She looked at the flares, was about to get moving again, but then she had a thought. She looked at the creature, it's back to the few flares that were burning in the woods, and then she remembered the creature's eyes, how black they were, as if they didn't have irises. What... could... no, that would be something that would only make sense in movies. She looked down at the flare again, her indecision lasting only a second longer, the memory of those eyes that had stared at her the first night driving her to further action. She had to take a chance.

She picked up the flare and with axe in hand, ran past her friends, even as Sosa and Jackson joined up with First Squad. They yelled at her to slow down, but she kept running, praying she was right. She soon got to the battle, her own body being peppered by blood, got as close as she dared to the creature, held out the flare, grabbing the end that lighted it, and yelled, "Hey, asshole!"

The creature turned, Second Platoon's platoon leader dead in its hand, its black eyes turning to the girl that challenged it, and Jenny lit the flare. The end lit in a blinding flash, the light hitting the creature's retinas. It screamed, dropping the dead Lt. Silverheels and its hands at its eyes, screaming in pain, unable to see. She rushed forward, grabbing her axe as she did so, and brought the burning flare to the creature's pull over hoodie. The material it was made out of burned in an instant. Within a moment, it was on fire, and now the creature slashed out, Jenny barely managing to skip back. Then Hickman, Jackson, and twelve others armed with carbines came forward, the ones behind the vampire got out of the way, and the fourteen soldiers opened fire on the creature. It screamed, its pants now on fire, being pushed back by the concentrated fire directed at it. It couldn't heal this time, the fire negating whatever healing factor it had before being set ablaze. Jenny saw an opportunity and got between Hickman and a Sergeant she didn't know, raised her axe over her head and behind her back, then throwing it end over end at the creature's chest. By some miracle of god, it landed true, the blade sinking into its chest and popping its heart, its blood supply spurting from the blade, spraying pass the fire.

It screamed, and then it fell, its body turning into so much burning meat. Hickman yelled to hold fire as Jenny rushed forward, getting the axe out of the charring corpse, which smelled like dead, decayed pork, before the wooden handle could burn. She turned to the assembled rifle men, and raised it in triumph, and the surviving solders roared battle cries. Victory was theirs. Hamish and Garcia sneaking a kiss, the others too distracted to notice.

It was over, and the jubilation of their victory was short lived, though before it died, Lt. Perry got it to last just a moment longer when he said, "I guess that's one for Hamish, and two for Dang." It didn't last because all around them were dozens of dead, human bodies.

"How many did we lose?!" yelled Perry.

The surviving NCOs got a quick number. SFC Alibudbun, who

was the senior surviving NCO, came forward, his face devoid of that cheer it usually had.

"Sixty men, sir," said Alibudbun.

"Sixty..." began Perry, but he stopped, biting his lips to keep from crying, the surviving soldiers around him. First Squad was together, Hamish and Garcia holding hands, nobody noticed, for they were grieving. Sergeant Sengel was among the dead, drained of his blood. Third Platoon's original 40 was now down to twenty. Perry managed to hold back tears, sighed, and said, "SPC Dang, Hamish, come forward." They did, he looked at them, and said, "I need to know each way you killed them."

Jenny called to Hickman who came forward. Together, the three explained how they killed the vampires, as Hickman called them. Perry nodded, and said, "We know they don't like bright light, and beheading does good, as well, to take them down."

"Okay, go back to your squad."

They rejoined Sergeant Garcia, Sosa, and Jackson.

Taking deep breaths, he and the only other surviving Lieutenant, Lt. Rima, an Argentina-American, about 4 foot 8, and shoulder length hair, stood together. He called SFC Alibudbun and SSG Lee, and they came together, whispering for several seconds. When it was done, Lt. Perry called, "Okay, grab your packs, we are moving out."

Before the moans could come, he yelled, "If those things come back tonight, I won't be caught with our pants down again! We move until first light and then drop our packs. We sleep in the day and move at night. I know it sucks, but I won't lose any more men tonight."

"What about the dead?!" yelled Sergeant Miller.

Perry again breathes deeply and said, "We'll come back for them. We get to the town first. The battalion needs us. Let's move."

Jenny and the others grabbed their packs, and started to march, tired and praying for an early sun. Everyone looked back at their fallen battles. Soldiers swore an oath to never leave a fallen comrade, and what they were doing was a betrayal of that oath and one that would haunt the survivors for the rest of their days. May God forgive them.

CHAPTER TWELVE

Final Pushes

"It is not faith that distinguishes our real leaders. It is doubt.

Their ability to overcome it."

— Guillermo del Toro and Chuck Hogan, *The Night Eternal*

Orson stood waiting as his clan sprinkled the earth they were buried in on the ground, and when done, lay down and sank into the earth as if the ground were quicksand. The sun was only a half an hour off, but he was still waiting for Cheech and Chong in the fading darkness. They were not back yet. He started with 39 vampires this feeding; he was now down to thirty-four. He couldn't understand. Those two should had been back by now, and well feed.

Legwang, the only other still awake on this cold, dark morning, came up and said, "They are dead."

"No," said Orson, "The humans couldn't kill the two of them."

"They killed three of us in the camp tonight," said Legwang, "they are adapting. Tomorrow, if you are so inclined to attack again, we will lose more."

"They can't..."

"You are a tarantula fighting an ant colony. You're bigger and stronger, but the ants outnumber you, billions to one. Why do you think we stay on the edges of humanity? Because in the end, we can't overwhelm them."

Orson snorted, and said, "Well, tomorrow, I'll just make more."

Legwang turned to him, his eyes glinting with humor and distaste for the being before him.

"Pray tell, more what?"

"More of our kind."

Legwang threw his head back and laughed, his voice echoing throughout the forest. His mirth confused Orson, who then realized he had never heard Legwang laugh before.

"Fool," he laughed, his Elvis style clothing shaking with him, "You're a fool."

"What so funny?"

Legwang turned to him, an awful leer on his face.

"How many humans have you turned into vampires in your lifetime?"

Orson was shocked by the question, and soon even realized he was shocked by the answer. In over a hundred years of his existence, he realized he had never turned one human.

"None. But I've seen it done. All they have to do is feed on my blood."

Legwang again was caught into another round of humorless

laughter, his black eyes bulging, and he said, "I lived for over 12,000 years, how many vampires have I turned?"

Orson shrugged, not knowing the answer.

"Not a single one."

Orson was shocked, his fanged mouth dropping open, unable to hide his surprise. Twelve thousand years, and he never turned a human? How?

"Why?"

"Only an Elder can change a human into a vampire." he said, laughing, "Ever wonder why nobody but the Elder could ever change anyone?"

Orson's mind was racing. Surely, somebody in the clan had to have changed a human. Someone. But he couldn't think of an instance were a human was changed outside of the Elder doing it himself.

"So, how can I do it?" he begged the answer.

Legwang smiled and said, "Only by drinking the blood of an Elder, all of it. Only two vampires in known history have achieved this, for drinking from an Elder isn't easy. Elders are the strongest of our kind, but they are also not the dumbest, like you are."

Orson's shock was replaced by rage, and he faced Legwang fully, and said, "I may not be an Elder, but I am still leading this clan, and if you don't want to die, you will take those words back."

Legwang's beautiful face was still smiling, and he said, "I wouldn't challenge me if I were you. I have done nothing to you because if I had, the others would have me, but you alone, are no match for me."

Orson slashed out with his claws, meaning to rip that pretty face off of Legwang's skull. Not seeing how, Legwang blocked the claw going for him, and sent Orson flying through a tree, the tall willow falling over, and Legwang easily stepped out of the path of the trunk. Orson was back on his feet in seconds, going in for another slash, but Legwang easily dodged each attack without needing to block the blows. He let Orson continue to slash for about fifty more seconds, then slipped behind him, kicking the back of Orson's knee, forcing him down, and then Legwang locked both his arms in a steel grip, and bent and whispered in his ears.

"You know what, even if you kill the remaining humans tomorrow night, you will never give the humans back the fear they once had. Do you want to know why? Because you and the others are only driven by your blood lust. You never need to adapt or create. You are only driven to feed, as we all are. You waste your longevity on your need to feed and wondering where your next meal will come from. However, 12,000 years of existence has taught me this: humans, though short of life, always adapt and improve themselves. They create, they build, and their fear left them long ago. Down at that camp, they don't have garlic, or silver. They only have wood, and yet they have killed six of us so far. Tomorrow, even if you kill all in the camp and kill all those in the woods, they will kill more of us tomorrow, for they will learn from their loss, and keep fighting.

"I have learned much from the cattle as you call them. Martin Luther King, Gandhi, Churchill, the Borgias, Attila the Hun, Aristotle, Adolf Hitler, just to name a few from the most recent history. I watched Jesus nailed to the cross. I watched Genghis Khan raid Eurasia, and the humans overwhelming the old magic users. They are the masters of this world; they and their deep, vast culture. Maybe one day there will be room for creatures like us again. I sensed a wakening when we were in Leon County, but in order to survive, we must improve ourselves. It took me 3000 years to learn this truth and I learned from the humans. I am no longer driven by blood, save to survive. I learn from their words. The Elder was learning as well, but when you took him, you cut off the head of the clan."

"Kill me," snarled Orson, "kill me and be done."

Legwang whispered and said, "I don't need to, and I won't. We can't let these humans survive and unleash the hunters again. I let you live to clean up your mess. I want one thing though."

"What?" gasped Orson, desperate to be freed of this teenage looking creature.

"I want to know what you did with the Elder's coffin."

Orson felt more pain, his arms being removed from their sockets. He yelled, "The Black River, it floats down it!"

"Fool," snarled Legwang. "Clean your mess up, and when I return with the Elder, I'll even let you try and drink from him. It will be your only chance, for when we return, he will destroy you. After that, he will kill the others, and he will rebuild the clan with me. Goodbye, you fool."

Orson fell to the ground, pushed himself up, turned and saw Legwang was gone. Fear pulsed through him, but the sun was not far off, so he sprinkled his earth on the ground, laid down, and sunk into it, realizing he was now down to 33 vampires to fight tomorrow. He would lose more than he or Legwang would expect tomorrow night.

***

Colonial Norris marched into 549's command building, acknowledged Staff Duty who called attention, and went down the hall to the briefing room. Captain Choi was in there, as were two other officers, including Lt. Miranda, and a three NCO's on rear guard. They all went to attention for her.

"Relax," she said, her blonde hair tied in a knot behind her head. "Any word?"

"No ma'am," said Captain Choi, he and the others sitting back at the conference table, Colonel Norris sitting on the opposite side, "we have a TMP waiting for a goa..."

"I got a call from General Bryant," she said, her face twisted in discuss, "No TMP are to be sent to Sight Indigo for another twenty-four hours."

What?! was pretty much everyone's response, and Norris had to raise her hands to quiet them.

"I know, it is bull, but this is a lawful order now."

"Ma'am, we are willing to risk our ranks to go out there," said Choi, trying to control the anger in his voice, "We haven't heard anything from the field Mission for 36 hours or more. I'm willing to risk my rank for this."

"So am I," said Norris, "but the fact is we don't know what's going on. It could just be a malfunction. We have to stay calm. As for the General, I have an idea."

She pulled out her cellphone and said, "Lt. General McCoy is here in New York, investigating an incident in Leon County Michigan."

"I thought the investigation involved the Michigan State National Guard and Fort Hood," said a Lt. Levi, a short man, half black and half white with cauliflower ears. "Why is he here?"

"He just stopped in to visit his father in the hospital. I'll see if he can help."

"How?" asked Captain Choi.

"Give me ten minutes, and I'll let you know."

She took a deep breath, and dialed, feeling like a traitor to her division commander. She dialed.

Lt. General McCoy left the hospital in Syracuse. He had a tear he was holding back in his eyes. His father had Leukemia and was nearing the end. His mother hadn't left his side once. He didn't want to either, but he still was looking over the Leon County incident.

Taking off his face mask, he walked down the road to the black car across from him. COVID fucked everything up. Two weeks of quarantine, come on, this was crazy. He just wasn't allowed to say it. His father was now isolated in a bubble, fear of the virus taking what was left of his life. What life? Hooked up to machines as the cancer slowly ate away at him. Fuck that, let him die in peace. He was just glad he had a 'Do Not Resuscitate Order' now. That was not how an old General like his dad should die. Let nature take its course.

He reached the car, his dress blues keeping the autumn cold off him, and just got in the back seat, telling his driver to head to the airport when the call came in. Pulling out his phone, he answered.

"General McCoy."

"General, it's Colonel Cathy Norris."

For a moment, he couldn't place her, but then, raking his head, he remembered. Cathy had been his XO when he was a company commander in Fort Lee.

"Cathy, how you doing?"

"Good, sir. Sir, I need you to overturn the order of General Bryant."

A look of concern came over his face as his driver headed for the airport. That was a tall request.

"May I ask why?" asked McCoy.

Norris explained the situation quickly as possible, and the

more she told, the more concerned he got.

"Wait, you're saying he ordered all cellphones to be taken away, including the Battalion commander?"

"Yes, sir," she said.

"And hasn't allowed anyone to find out what happened, in fact ordering nobody in the rear guard to go and see if they need help, in fact the opposite."

"Yes, sir."

McCoy rubbed his forehead. He knew Brigadier General Bryant, in fact, was invited to his retirement party next week. This wasn't like him. He was always for the soldiers and cutting them off like that wasn't right and not like him at all.

"One second," said McCoy who said, "SPC Oliver, reset out destination to Fort Drum."

"Sir," said his driver, pulling over and putting the new destination into WAZE, "but I feel like I should point out, sir, you are due in Michigan tonight."

"Put a cap on it. Call my aide, he should be already out there and tell him to start the investigation without me. I will be there soon as I can."

"Yes, sir."

He went back to his phone, "Cathy I'm on my way. Should be there in a couple of hours. Send some guys up there. Ask them to use civilian vehicles. Those kids have been cut off for too long, let's help them."

"Thank you, sir."

McCoy hung up and then called his boss, who reported to his boss, who came back and told McCoy to go check the situation in Fort Drum out. American bureaucracy at its finest. Helped having more stars on your shoulders than most.

Cathy hung up and turned to Choi, "Get a couple of guys in

a car. Get them up there to Site Indigo, ASAP."

Captain Choi nodded, and said, "Okay, someone sign out a TMP and..."

"No," said Norris, "Send some guys in their civilian vehicles. We are not wasting any more time."

"I'll go," said Lt. Miranda, standing, her ebony face set in determination.

"I'll go, too," said SSG Carter.

"Good luck," muttered Choi. "Drove with Miranda once, and that was enough. She got some road rage."

There was a much needed chuckle. Relief was in. They were finally going to do something about this strange situation that was a shit show from the start.

"Go, now, and I'll call the state police," said Choi, "have them help you."

The two nodded and headed out of the building. After they were gone, PVT Lawrence, who was the Staff Duty runner today, came and said, "Sir, we are getting something on the radio."

They stood as a group and ran to the hall.

"Five-four-nine, 549, this is ECP Forward," said SPC Gentry for the third time as Colonel Swarts and Major Dong stood nervously behind them, Deraps keeping an eye on the makeshift radio. They spent the last day cobbling it together, finding what intact components they could find from the smashed radios. It was not in a green case, but was a pile of wires and circuits, its transponder cracked, and sparking. They were holding their breaths, praying to god this would work. This was their one chance. Deraps and Gentry had worked on this even during the attack. There were less than a hundred and forty survivors, the bodies still outside where they laid slain. Too concerned about the few survivors, Chaplin Wright had put them into the trucks they were now using as morgues. The large refrigeration unit was already full of the bodies of the dead; the thick metal walls, only muting the smell of decaying flesh.

The creatures, fuck it, Swarts was now just calling them vampires, their dead bodies, the three they got last night, had burned to ash when the sun rose, the smell of dead bodies clotting the air, making the living feel sick. It was ten o'clock, and the camp had been even more condensed. A single tent was all that was needed now to house and sleep those who could still fight. This had to work, it had to. Come on 514, where are you?

A voice came through after the fourth attempt. It crackled, static sound of a voice sounding as sweet as an angel's kiss at that moment. Deraps nearly sobbed.

Gentry handed the radio's receiver over to Colonel Swarts, who took it gingerly, the telephone wire held together with tape and prayer, who said, "Five-four-nine, past day and a half, we have been attacked by unknown combatants. There are over six hundred dead. I sent the 514 company to get help, but so far, we haven't gotten anything from them. They were heading to Malone. We need evac. Send choppers, Roger?"

He let go of the radio's side button, listening. Then...

"ECP For, repe...please say ag..."

It was cutting out then, the sparking on the transceiver made a large, cracking sound, and smoke filled the tent, the circuitry catching on fire. Major Dong put it out with a fire extinguisher. Pulling the pin, he sprayed, with white cloud coming from extinguisher putting it out.

Deraps fell on his rear, his hands on his face, and cried, "We are going die, you hear me, we are going to die."

"Get him out of here, take him to the Chaplin."

Major Dong did, picking him up and rushing him out. SPC

Gentry just sat there, unable to move. Swarts prayed that enough got through.

What was heard at the Staff Duty radio, which SSG Riva was working was, "Five-four-nine... atta... six hundred... 514... haven't got... Malone. We ne... Roger?"

Colonel Norris blood ran cold when she heard six hundred. She hoped that wasn't lives.

She turned to Captain Choi.

"Tell Lt. Miranda to hurry her ass up. I'll try to get some choppers from aviation. Call me when the General arrives.

"Yes ma'am."

She left, running.

Swarts walked outside the camp, soldiers working on the defenses, and he knew if they had a chance, most would try and run for it. He didn't blame them and was on the verge of making that an option. He walked across the field, looking at the dead bodies of his men and women. He passed the corpse of his CSM, his friend, and felt the tears coming. He held them.

He found the man he was looking for, Captain Wright, his bald head sweating as he did last rights, his uniform fresh, but his hands stained red.

He walked up to the Chaplin, who was on his knees and said, "Can we talk?"

The Chaplin, seeing him, nodded and stood with a Bible in hand. They walked pass pale and sick looking soldiers, many unable to believe what was happening. They were dying, and accepting they weren't getting help. They reached the Chaplin's small tent. They entered. Two chairs were in front of the Chaplin's cot, and they sat.

"What do you need, sir?" asked Wright, his eyes concerned.

Swarts put his arms on his upper legs, leaning forward, not

looking at the Chaplin, and said, "I don't know if I can get my men out of this. I sit here, watching them desperately try and make some kind of defense for the camp, but I see it as almost hopeless. I'm tempted to tell them just to run so some might have a chance to live. I've done many tours in the Middle East, and I've lost men and women before, but not like this. I don't know what the point of fighting this is anymore. I'm asking them to stay when the more logical idea is to get them out of here, but that may cause more death."

Wright was silent for a long time, almost two minutes, looking at the Colonel, a blank expression. Then he spoke.

"It's too late to run, sir. If they run, yes, some might some survive, but they are broken men, their hearts shattered by what they have witnessed. We stand here, and know it is hopeless, but if we make it every man for himself; they will be broken and won't be able to live with what they had done."

Swarts rubbed his face, not liking the Chaplin's answer, holding back tears. "So, what do I do?"

"You ever see the movie 'Glory'?" he asked.

Colonel Swarts finally looked at him and shook his head.

"It was about the 545th Massachusetts Infantry Regiment. It was the second all black regiment made in the Union Army. It was decimated during the second battle of Fort Wagner. Anyways, there was a part in that movie, and I later was able to verify this with historical records, that Jefferson Davis had issued an order that any black enlisted man, and the white officers that they served under, were captured, they would be put to death. Colonel Shaw, the regimental commander, realizing this would put these, as he would put it back in his day, so forgive my verbiage, negro soldiers, at undo risk, and gave them an offer to leave the military if they chose to, no questions asked. The next day, not one black volunteer left the regiment. They were fighting for more than the Union, you see. They were fighting for their people's freedom. That meant more to them then a death threat meant to scare them."

He smiled at the strange look on Swarts' face. It was a look of understanding.

"I don't know what these things are. I am prone to call them vampires, but who knows, and in the end, it doesn't matter. But we managed to kill four of them here. I don't know if we will get help or not before the sun goes down, but I do know this: those things, those vampires, are a risk to every man, woman, and child in these states. Don't matter the race, creed, or religion. We might not survive, but if we stand and take as many of those bastards with us as we can, it will be a sacrifice worth having. Our families back at Fort Drum will be safer if we even manage to kill even one more of these things. That is what is going to keep your men going. Trust me, they'd put themselves in harm's way if you told them you could shoot down the coronavirus. They'd go into the infected regions and do it. That's what they need: a reason to keep going."

Swarts heard these words and realized what he was getting at. His men and women were soldiers. They would fight to the last if they had a reason. They would face down those black eyed, pointed ear creatures and strike back if they had a reason. He stood and said, "Tell all surviving command teams I want all survivors here in an hour."

The Chaplin stood and said, "Yes, sir."

He left and Swarts stood strong, ready to face the darkness.

***

The 514 was on its last legs at noon. They were tired, had

covered over 50 miles, and were praying that the smell of copper would go away. Everyone had blood on their outfits, staining them, the red bright against the brown and green of the OCPs. And they were all so tired, all 79 of them.

After checking the map, Lt. Perry nodded at Sosa, who had taken over land-nav duties and said, "Okay, people, bedtime. Let's get in the woods and try and sleep for a few hours."

"Uhhhhhhhh," was the collective response as they moved into the tree line and collapsed. Knock out time.

First Squad got together and collapsed together, going to their butts on the ground, dropping packs and weapons and soon were all lying down. Jenny felt blisters under her feet, and they were hurting. Her back was sore and stiff. Madam Roseta would have a field day with her when she got back, telling her she had to keep herself healthy if she ever wanted to become a professional dancer. At this moment, it didn't seem as important as trying to get a few hours of sleep.

Hamish was lying next to Sergeant Garcia. Hickman lied near them on Hamish's other side. He moaned.

"God, are we there yet?"

"Twenty more miles," moaned Garcia, who was letting go of her hard girl stance and letting herself relax.

"Twenty," moaned Hickman, "I never want to march again."

"Sergeant," said Hamish, looking over at her, "I think I'll take that leave. After all this shit, and if we survive, I think I can handle my father. Plus, I think I need a vacation after this. Barn raising was easy compared to the last two nights."

Jenny snorted, and said, "If we survive tonight, I'm taking early ETS as well Sergeant."

"Just put in the paperwork and I will sign it," chuckled Garcia. "Think I'll do it too."

"Man," moaned Jackson, "this is worse than Korea. I miss the Juicy Girls."

"SHARP," moaned Sosa, jokingly, elbowing Jackson in the ribs.

"Can't blame you for being grumpy," said SFC Alibudbun, who came out of nowhere. He looked down at the remnants of First Squad, his eyes flicking to Hamish and Sergeant Garcia, but not saying anything; he would just lay down. He had a bruised eye and was breathing hard, but he said, "So, I got two vampire slayers in my company."

"That's the term we're using," groaned Hickman, "vampire?"

"I guess so. Demon seems too melodramatic."

"Huh," groaned Jenny, "why didn't we cover this one during basic?"

She looked at the sky as the chitchat started to tire out, with Jackson already snoring. The light at noon was the brightest, but to her, it seemed like it was just getting dimmer and dimmer. Every minute, the safety of the sun would soon be lost and those things...those...those vampires would be back. More would die. They'd send their pointed eared killers and mow through more soldiers.

Lt. Perry came over and said, "I wish I could say I was here to talk defense, but honestly, I just want to hang with my best squad."

He fell over, landing on his back, moaning in pain for a moment, and reaching under his back, removing a rock that was there, and threw it away.

"Well," said Hickman, "when the big wigs are with you, you know it's bad."

"Ah, come on," said Hamish, nearly falling asleep, "we got

three in our company, that's more than any other I bet."

"Wonder how they are doing?" muttered Alibudbun.

"Shitty I bet," said Garcia.

"We got a strategy," groaned Perry, "and we know we can kill them."

"Problem is, they move to fast." muttered Jenny. "If we could just get them cornered, we could take them on better. You saw it last night. If they can't run, they are easier to kill."

Hickman, after that, sat up, his eyes showing he was wide awake.

"What if we did corner them?"

All eyes in the group were upon them, shocked at how determined he was.

"What if we draw them into one area, thinking their being attacked. What if we lure them to that area, keep rifle men on the opposite side and then we flare them. We concentrate fire, then..."

He grabbed a stick and drew his plan out, using lines, an X to represent the soldiers and an O the vampires. Sleep forgotten, they watched in interest.

"How would you draw them?" asked Alibudbun.

"We got any blanks?"

"I do." Jackson who awoke with the plan being formed. "Ain't going to be charged with losing them."

"I got a few," said Sosa.

"Well," said Hickman, the idea blossoming, "we use them to draw them in."

"That will put the shooters at risk," pointed out Perry.

Hickman bit his lip, thinking, then a look of excitement came to his face. He looked like a much younger man; all his troubles driven away by this one idea. This caused the others to look hopeful.

"We got any 5-50 cord?"

"SSG Lee brought a roll," pointed out Alibudbun, seeing what he was thinking, and so did Jenny.

"We tie the 5-50 cord around the triggers. No risk to the shooters."

Hickman stood. "I need to rifle. Do a test."

Hickman, the remnants of First Squad, Alibudbun, and Perry all stood. Alibudbun went over to SSG Lee, who gave him forty feet of 5-50 cord, the green string that was used for repairs. After burning the cut endings, Alibudbun handed it to Hickman, who tied it around his and Jackson's triggers very carefully. Then he through the other end around a tree branch about fifteen feet up, using a rock tied to the other end to do so. Hamish caught it, and he pulled the string out, tightening the end.

When everyone cleared, and when Hickman took the string and nodded to Lt. Perry, he yelled, "Fire in the hole!"

Hickman pulled the string, lifting the two rifles, they're going in the air, the weapons on auto, and firing three test rounds, the sound causing everyone to jump away, but, seeing no danger, went back to sleep. Hickman lowered the weapons, and they stopped firing.

SFC Alibudbun said, "Hickman, if this works, then I'm putting you in for a metal."

Hickman shrugged and said, "Make that a bottle of Jim Beam, and we will call it even."

Jenny who was excited, kissed Hickman right on the cheek, who blushed but smiled.

Hamish and Garcia laughed, Jackson muttering, "I want my rifle back."

But, sleeping near the string, First Squad of Third Platoon felt a little more hopeful.

Miranda and Carter drove down the highway, getting off US-11 N, and getting onto NY-11 B N. Carter's balls felt like they were being sent back up the way to where they originally were before they dropped and were being squeezed like a vice. Miranda drove like a NASCAR driver, and he swore they were going to die over a hundred times. She seemed to avoid crashes by inches in her vintage mustang, and one near miss with a semi convinced SSG Carter that this woman had to be psychic somehow, knowing where and how to swerve.

They got to the exit to get onto NY-11 BN and drove down for several miles until they came to a sudden stop. The road was blocked, traffic being halted. Miranda looked at the clock. It was only 1300 hours.

"What the fuck?" she cursed, getting out her car at the stopped traffic. She started walking between the lanes caused by the cars, lining up and honking.

"Ma'am," called Carter, "Lieutenant, I don't think..."

She was already out of earshot.

"Shit, shit, shit."

Carter got out of the car and followed, drawing the eyes of the civilians, the two in OCPs, running through traffic. They came to two cops, a barrier, and a construction site, three workers working on a hole in the road.

"What the hell is going on here?!" she yelled. Carter winced. She may be a Lieutenant in the United States Army, but being a black woman yelling at two white cops in masks, Carter sensed trouble.

The younger one, a pimply sandy blonde kid stepped up and said, "Get in your car lady, right now."

Lt. Miranda whirled on the pimpled covered cop and said,

"What did you call me, boy?"

The boy's hand on his gun side started to move, and Carter was about to step in when the older of the two cops put a hand on him.

"Dwight, calm your ass down. Go back to the barricade."

"But that bitch..."

"Can turn you into a pretzel if she wanted to. Go back."

The older man stayed put as the pimpled cop stepped away, grumbling.

"Sorry about that," said the older man, "I'm officer Calaway; how can I help you?"

"Officer, we trying to get to Site Indigo. It's a training facility thirty miles south of Malone. We have been out of contact for 39 hours or so. We have been sent to see if everything is alright."

Calaway raised his eyes, removing the mask covering his mouth.

"Do you expect foul play?"

"I don't what's going on, all we got about an hour ago was a garbled transmission that didn't tell us anything. We need to go there, and you're blocking the road."

Calaway sighed and said, "I'm sorry ma'am, but we got a burst gas pipeline and we can't risk it exploding. It's connected to several towns in the region."

Miranda's eyes opened, too shocked to speak. Carter stepped up, "Sir, is there any way we can turn around?"

Calaway shook his head, "Not here. And it's going to take at least five hours to repair the pipeline."

"Damn it," swore Miranda.

"I could call the station at Malone; they could send someone and report back."

The two soldiers stared at each other, shocked. Why didn't

they think of that?

"Please," said Miranda, who in a sudden burst of emotion, thanked him with a kiss on the lips. Carter's jaw dropped. Calaway blushed. The state trooper turned and walked back to the cruiser, a smile on his lips, hadn't had been kissed randomly by a beautiful woman in a long time. He sat down, and picked up his phone, and dialed.

Patrisha Backster was once called Mama Seita as her stage name when she worked porn. But when she moved to Malone, she fell in love with the town. She became a dispatcher for the local police unit and was the envy of every other department. Her long, blonde highlighted hair, her perfect red lips, her long eyelashes, rolling hips, those innocent eyes, she had more job offers then she could count. But she loved this town, leaving the porn industry for it. It had a small-time vibe with a lot to offer. She loved her job, which involved helping people.

The phone rang, and she picked it up.

"Malone PD," she said in her natural, honey voice that made men beg for her favor.

"Patrisha, it's Calaway."

Patrisha turned, her large breasts barely contained by her bra. She said, "What you need, sweetie?"

"Hey, can you get some guys to a place called Site Indigo. Got a coordinate I can send you via text. Got a couple of soldiers saying that they have a battalion they lost contact with almost two nights ago."

Her phone buzzed and she looked at it. Calaway's number appeared and showed a text message. She opened it, numbers appearing indicating a grid coordinate. She nodded, put it into WAZE, and saw it was less than forty minutes away. It was on back roads but should be alright.

"Sure, honey," said Patrisha, "I'll get Dean on it."

"Who?"

"Dean, you know, the new guy. Came down about three months ago from Belaphone, up in Michigan."

"Oh, yeah, thanks."

"Welcome, honey."

She went to the radio and called up Dean's patrol car after shooting him a text.

"Hey Dean, I'm texting you some grid coordinates."

A crackle over the radio, then... "Okay, got them, not far from where I'm...hey, some of that is back road, middle of nowhere."

"Sorry, sugar," said Patrisha, "But Frank is on the Southside today, and Burns is handling some early drunks. Coronavirus, you know."

A sigh came over the radio but responded with a, "Alright, I'm heading out now."

Patrisha smiled and said, "Thanks, sugar."

She smiled and relaxed hands over her head stretching her ample bosom and smiling. She then called back Calaway and said, "Kid's on his way, honey."

"Thanks, sweetie."

Calaway looked up at the two soldiers and said, "I got them to send a patrol car, he should be able to get there in a few hours."

"Okay," said Miranda.

"As for you two, I'm going to have one of our patrol cars escort you to a turnaround point. You will have to go down and around, and it will take you a few hours to get there, but hopefully, my guy will be able to find out what is going on and if you leave your numbers, we will contact you as soon as possible, that way Fort Drum can respond before you get there."

They gave him their numbers, and a patrol car lead them down to the turnaround point meant for emergency vehicles, and they took off, hopeful. Like many things that seem to be going good though, things will often end with the day being ruined. This was one of those days.

Colonel Swarts stepped out of the Chaplin's tent at 1400, finally knowing what he was going to say, and marched out to the remains of the 549 Support Battalion. And 138 were standing before him in a semi-circle. He had learned from First Sergeant Hicks that Captain Jones had succumbed to infection an hour ago, and he saw his remaining soldiers looking hopeless. He looked at each of his men, each one, and didn't see the battalion anymore. He only saw soldiers, men and women knowing that they were most certainly facing a fight they couldn't win. The slow moving and dimming sun slowly ticking off the hours until nightfall, when the, finally admitting to themselves their names, vampires, would come back, and kill what remained.

Swarts looked at them, Major Dong standing with him, his face set in a face of determination. He took a breath and said, "I know, as do you, this seems like a losing battle. What makes it worse is we are home. Things like this are only supposed to happen overseas. Things like this don't happen at home."

Everyone looked still down cast, not yet carrying about what was being said.

"But things like this do happen at home. The coronavirus, the protest for George Floyd, the divide that hits our nation every day, the election fight. We know we have the power to crush it, but we can't. The American people have a right to change society for the better, and it's the roll of the military to change with society. Sometimes we lead that change. Before Korea, we segregated our own Army, and before that, before the civil war, there were entire groups of people we didn't recognize as Americans. Blacks, the indigenous population, Asians. Before that, to serve in the military, you had to hide the fact you were homosexual to fight for your country. The change started with don't ask, don't tell, then it changed where who you love didn't matter, just the want to serve your country."

The eyes of the 139 men and women, though still lost and hopeless, looked up, a hint of a need for hope coming into their eyes, long lost two nights ago. Swarts knew he had them and had to keep going before it was lost again.

"But there is also an oath, no matter if you're enlisted or commissioned, that all soldiers do take. Protect the United States from all threats, foreign and domestic. The social injustice now taking place in America isn't a threat to the United States. That is a progression need for the United States of America. It's the only way this great nation improves. But these creatures, they are a threat to the United States. They don't care for our right to life, and have spent two days whittling down our numbers, feeding on us, and taking away from us. If they are willing to do that to us, then they are willing to do that to every man, woman, child, no matter the creed, religion, or race you are, they will be willing to attack every single person here at home."

Understanding came to their eyes. Click: Swarts had them, the gleam of the coming hope returning to their eyes. Swarts voice rose, a tone of determination entering it.

"I have left a journal of everything that has happened tonight, including all the names of the current dead. The only ones left out are those of the 514 that left to get help. Those names include all assembled before me. I pray that each and every one of us gets rescued tonight, and we are able to go home to our love ones. But if tonight is our time, then let's take as many of those bastards with us to hell. They threaten our homes, our loved ones. So, let's make them pay for every life they take tonight. Let them know that they are fighting the 549 and we will make them pay for threatening our home."

The soldiers roared, a new determination and power going through them, brought out by their commanding officer. They raised rifles and other weapons, wanting rescue no longer but to fight.

"The Chaplin will stand here and if you have a final note you wish to give, give it. As for the rest of us, well, I bet we all know and expect these things are vampires, so, let's hope we can use that against them."

"I've got a ton of Garlic powder!" yelled the one remaining cook, "We can put it on the stakes."

"I got some silver!" yelled the Chaplin, who just came up, carrying two candle holders used in Jewish faith, "Let's use it."

"Shoot them while they're in the air!" yelled one soldier, "We don't have much ammo left, and I doubt we are ever getting that ammo truck back, but hell, it worked once last night."

"Alright!" yelled Swarts. "We've got three hours. Let's make them count."

"Hooah!" they yelled, and Swarts knew, weather they survived or not, tonight, this fight was going to be different. This night, they were going to make those bastards pay for every drop of blood they spilled.

CHAPTER THIRTEEN

Count Down

"Well, screw him. I'd tried my best."
— Charlaine Harris, *Dead Until Dark*

It was 1500 came when General McCoy finally arrived at 549's HQ. Colonel Norris was still there, her own Brigade duties for now taken over by her own XO and CSM. He walked in, his three stars seemed to stand out on their own on his OCPs, pressed and professional, his tan boots seeming to gleam, didn't get the attention they deserved at first. This was because they were both at the radio, the NCO saying, "Try a different frequency."

The Soldier responding, "That could make things worse Sergeant."

The NCO responded with, "Understood, but still try."

This lack of attention at the front of HQ would have normally caused this General to lose this temper, but with the situation being what it was, he understood and had accommodated for their dedication. He cleared his throat, and both looked up, jaws dropping and faces looking red, and quickly going to attention. The NCOIC was about to call the building to attention, but Lt. General McCoy raised his hand.

"No need. I believe your Battalion's Brigade Commander is here."

"Yes, sir," said the NCOIC, a Sergeant Reed, "she is in the briefing room with Captain Choi, commander of the rear guard."

McCoy nodded. "Carry on but remember to keep eyes at the front as well as the radio."

"Yes, sir," they both said as McCoy walked away down the hall, him wearing a face mask because of coronavirus. He took it off when he reached the briefing room. Colonel Norris, Captain Choi, and the Acting CSM, SGM Curry, were all listening to a phone call from SSG Carter.

"We just got on the secondary route. We will be there in about three hours."

"The gas line is still under repairs on the primary route?" asked Captain Choi, his face looking haggard.

"Yes, sir, but our state cop friend, Calaway, is keeping us updated with regular reports on the officer's progress to Site Indigo."

"What's taking him so long?" asked Colonel Norris, her face with a look of worry on it.

"Well, ma'am, he's taking a police cruiser on dirt and gravel. Not the best choice to travel on fast. Also, as you know, even with GPS, it's not easy to find your way to Site Indigo unless you know where to go. We didn't exactly design it with the hope that civilians would find it easily. But we hope he will beat us there."

Colonel Norris rubbed the bridge of her noise with her left hand, her right cupping her left shoulder. She did this in time of great stress or witnessing great stupidity. When she finished rubbing, she looked up and saw General McCoy at the door. She was about to call the room to attention when the General raised his hand and shook his head, indicating this was more important than acknowledgement of his presence.

"Okay," said Captain Choi, "continue your mission; be

careful."

"Yes, sir," said Carter, then hung up.

McCoy walked in and said, "So, we still haven't reached the Field Mission, yet?"

Captain Choi, who just noticed the General, went pale, the blood draining from his face, and was about to yell attentions, Curry already there on instinct, seeing the three star at the same time as Choi, but again, McCoy stopped them, saying, "Stuff it, ain't got time for formalities. Just give me the run down."

"So, far sir, the primary path we take to Site Indigo was cut off due to a gas line being damaged early in the morning so the two we sent out had to reroute."

McCoy nodded, "Sounds like someone is trying to keep us away from Site Indigo. I find it particularly unusual that it would get busted on the day we send out a search party. What about sending a chopper?"

Norris' face suddenly took on a pissed expression. "The Aviation Brigade commander, in his infinite wisdom, decided to have a mass TI on all its birds, the Colonel in charge saying a few days of silence and one garbled transmission wasn't enough to panic and send out a bi..."

"Do you have his number?"

Norris gave McCoy one Colonel Anderson's number. He dialed it. It answered on the sixth ring. Bad start. Rule number one in the military, don't make a General wait.

"Who's this?" snapped a deep voice over the phone, one dripping with stress and agitation, "I swear to Christ, if this is a fucking scam for my social security number, I'm going to hunt..."

"This is General McCoy," he said in a dangerously calm voice that instantly silenced the tirade full bird. Most Colonels and Lt. Colonels knew about Lt. General McCoy and had long learned to fear him.

"Oh, ahhhh, sir, how can I…"

"How soon can you have a bird fly over Site Indigo for a little look?"

Two seconds of silence then, "Well, sir, we are doing a TI and…"

"How soon?"

"Ahhhhh, including dispatches and inspections, two hours, minimum, sir."

"Thank you, Colonel Anderson, you are most helpful. Have some of your techs hook up their radios to the 549's HQ before you fly off. That will be all."

"Yes, sir, and may I say…"

McCoy hung up, and said, "Now, Colonel, you come with me for now. We are going to see General Bryant and check out what is going on."

Norris nodded and the two officers left, Captain Choi hearing a call to attention, with the General yelling back, "Carry on!"

General McCoy's car pulled up to 10 mountain's HQ, the building projecting the power of the 10th Mountain Division, its large and professional architecture hid the building moderating combat actions in every country 10 Mountain soldiers were deployed in. The highest ranking officers and NCOs of Fort Drum were in that building.

Colonel Norris often came here for briefings, but General McCoy had never, but flanked by two MPs that were requested by him, he marched to the building as if he owned it. Norris followed her stance more subordinate.

They entered the front doors where Division Staff Duty was, and they saw the 3-Star General coming, who quickly waved them down, not wanting them to call attention. He walked until he reached a directory sign, his mask covering his lower face, as it was for Norris and the two MPs with them. After locating the Division Commander's office, he went to the stairs and marched to the third floor. It was a pointed march, and he would not stop until its end. He was a determined man with a single mission which would be completed: to find out what was happening here at Fort Drum.

He reached the top floor, found the Commander's office, and flanked by his posse, marched in without hesitation. A secretary, an older civilian woman with steel gray hair, and a stern look, looked up and was about to say 'you can't go in there', when it died in her throat, seeing the 3-Star General going to the main office door. It was opened by hand by Lt. General McCoy as if it were his office, and not that of Brigadier General Bryant.

The MPs remaining outside, he and Colonel Norris entered the office. The room resembled that of a college professor more than one might think would be in an office of a war making US Army General. Its white walls were covered in degrees, certificates, and pictures of family, including grandchildren. The general sat at an oaken desk in a leather bound and professional swivel chair. The General was in it, and he looked up, indignant and about to yell at the intruder until he saw who it was. He quickly stood and went to attention for Lt. General McCoy. Three Stars on your chest always beats One Star.

"At ease, General," said McCoy, "relax."

"Sir," said General Bryant, "I didn't know you were coming here to Fort Drum. If I had known..."

"It's okay, Jim," said McCoy, using the first names they both used while in West Point. They were in the same class, and though McCoy won the honor's spot, Bryant was only a little behind.

Bryant smiled, noticing Colonel Norris behind him and said, "So, Roy, what brings you to my neck of the woods?"

McCoy sat on one of the two leather arm chairs; his elbows on the arms, his fingers intertwined. He had a pensive look, analyzing everything.

"Jim," he said, "I'd like to know, for the 549, why you took away their cellphones."

A paleness entered Bryant's face, and he seemed to become thinner with fear. Norris noticed this, holding her breath, or so she thought, not realizing her respiration was operating normally, she just didn't notice. She felt the General's agitation, though he kept a stone, cold poker face, despite his paleness.

"I believed that such an exercise would focus the soldiers on military training rather than the latest app they are using, sir. Sense basic has changed so much, we have to focus on harder training on our end to keep our soldiers alive."

McCoy nodded, "Ah huh, ah huh. Logical, during this pandemic, focusing on such training."

Fear crept up Norris' spine, like a flare, it hit her hard and fast. Was she about to get her back stabbed by her own mentor?

"The thing is," said McCoy, his eyes never moving from Bryant, "that you wrote a paper on the importance of keeping soldiers as connected as possible to their families. Until today, I could never conceive you giving such an order to your troops, especially to a battalion FTX. Such a mission is not even worth your notice. So why do you bring this up now?"

Bryant shifted, and Norris noticed that. It was barely noticeable, but it was there. Was he breaking?

"I'm also concerned," said General McCoy, "that you waited so long when you lost communication with the 549, and waited, what is it, almost 40 hours before trying to, A: establish communication, or B: try to figure out what is going on. That is unlike you, Jim."

Bryant again shifted, this time more noticeable, but said, "Roy, you know that communication loss is not uncommon overseas and..."

"And command has a duty to ensure what is going on and assist if it is needed," snapped McCoy, "Jim, what is the matter with you? I've known you for twenty-three years and this isn't like you."

"Sir," said Bryant, his voice having a failing masking note to it, "I believe the situation with your father has clouded your judgment, and you..."

McCoy stood, and at that moment, he appeared as a god, command, not to be question.

"Brigadier General Bryant, you are hereby relieved of your command upon investigation. When and if you..."

He didn't finish that sentence because, without warning, General Bryant flung himself across the desk, his hands reaching out, and tackling McCoy. The two collided and the leather chair came crashing to the floor, the chair breaking, the stuffing revealed as the leather tore under the two men's weight. But McCoy, having sixteen deployments and fourteen surgeries under his belt, he knew how to roll with the punches, and he did, taking both himself and Bryant, rolled in a circle. Bryant ended up on top, but instead of cold, calculated strikes, he was punching General McCoy like a street brawler in New York City, wild and sloppy, arms flinging down and blocked easily by McCoy.

Norris yelled, "MPs, get in here!"

The two Specialist MPs came in with the OCPs, and their Kevlar vest. Their mouths dropped, seeing the two Generals fighting on the floor, not sure who to help. Then both General McCoy and Colonel Norris yelled, "Get the one star off!" That answered that. Arresting a General, even one with just one star, was a career killer, unless you had some protection. The two Specialist grabbed General Bryant's arms, pinning him down, but he was still biting at them like a lunatic.

The stern looking civilian woman who acted as General Bryant's secretary, rushed in and screamed, "What are you..."

"Ma'am," Norris said quickly, "call an ambulance, the Division Commander is unwell."

The secretary ran and Norris turned to see General Roy McCoy squat in front of his friend and say, "Jim, what is going on?"

Suddenly, Bryant's shoulders slumped, and this strength going out of him, his face gaunt, his eyes seemingly distant, the MPs still holding his arms.

"He promised," moaned Bryant, "he promised."

"Who promised?" asked McCoy. "Who made you a promise, Jim?"

Bryant's eyes looked up, and they were blood shot, but didn't look away from his old friend.

"The pale man," he moaned, "the one with the black eyes."

Norris saw Bryant smile, and the dreamy quality that came over his face was almost eerie. It was as if he was having a dream while awake, one too good to wake up from.

"What did the pale man promise?" asked McCoy. "And what did he tell you to do?"

Bryant flushed, almost like a naughty child who was caught sneaking his hand into the cookie jar. "He promised everything he showed me in his eyes. Everything. Everything that me and Cathy wanted. No more military, just, her and me, our family, nothing else."

McCoy looked both compassionate and disgusted at the same time. Compassion from knowing how hard it was on spouses married to a career soldier; disgusted by him selling out his own men.

"What did you have to do?" he asked.

"Take away their cellphones," said Bryant.

"Why? What did the pale man want?"

"Too feed. I tried to refuse, but those eyes, they were so beautiful, and they promised me, they promised me."

Three paramedics came rushing up, a stretcher with them. They saw the Division Commander and they took over, Bryant not resisting, the last words he said making Norris feel sick. To feed? Six hundred... six hundred lives? No, please God no, not at home, not this.

McCoy watched them take away the General and he turned to Norris, the MPs following in the General. McCoy turned to Norris and said, "He had to have been controlled somehow. He had to. Jim, he never... he couldn't sell out his men like that. I know that man."

Tears were in his eyes, and Norris hugged her old mentor, he returning it. She saying, "I know, sir, I know, I can't believe he'd do this willingly."

He looked at the time: 1430 hours. A half an hour before sundown. A call came over the General's cell phone, and Norris released him so he could answer. It was Anderson.

"Yes," he said once he picked up the phone.

"Sir, we got a bird in ready to take off."

"Get them to Site Indigo and scramble some Chinooks. We need to get the men out of there."

"Their equipment as well?"

"Fuck the equipment," snapped McCoy, "The military can pay that bill. We need to get our troops. Now."

"Yes, sir."

The call ended; however, in the end, it would be pointless.

***

"Here they come!" yelled Sergeant Yo, a Thailand soldier who was on watch with 30 others, seeing the 30 now called vampires coming out of the tree line. They were yelling their Tasmanian devil calls, the horrible sound echoing in the darkness that had just come. As soon as the sun was gone, they were here. Tonight, they were not wasting time.

Colonel Swarts, Major Dong, and Chaplin Wright all came out to the killing zone, the remnants of their vehicles out there, the camp now smaller than last night, and the stake field more condensed. The tips covered in a paste mixed with garlic powder. The remaining stakes were in the hands of soldiers, holding them as if they were swords. Axes and pickaxes in the rest of the soldier's and officer's hands. Swarts looked at his men, and the look of anger and defiance was on their faces. He and all of the remaining 138 soldiers knew they were more than likely going to die tonight. They knew that this was going to be the end. But their end wasn't going to be that of fear. They were going to die with weapons in hand and take as many of those bastards with them as they could.

Swarts was proud of them, and he yelled, "Let's make them eat metal tonight!"

The soldiers roared, their battle calls hitting the vampire's calls with equal force, the sounds challenging each other. For a moment, the vampires paused. These men and women were not showing fear. They were showing a willingness to face the devil and smack him back to hell.

That pause gave time for Swarts to hand Chaplin Wright a lighter and the Chaplin saluted and said, "Sir, it's been a pleasure."

Swarts returned the salute and Wright turned to his tent. He knew what to do. Swarts and Dong turned, the vampires running at the defenses, then leaping over the C-wire. That was what they were waiting for. Tonight, only twenty soldiers were with carbines. Their mags were filled with the last of the ammo. Not needing orders, they opened fired on auto, firing three round bursts.

The vampires, still in the air, carefully planning their landings between the stakes were not ready for this, and five were hit. They fell to the ground uncontrollably. They landed on the garlic covered stakes, their bodies catching fire when they landed, the bright flames causing many to cover their faces, and the soldiers went in. Two more fell with their bodies impaled on stakes.

"For home!" yelled Swarts, as he and the others charged, the rifle men using up the last of their ammo, charging with them.

The vampires mowed them down when they reached them, taking out twenty in a second, but the warriors they faced did not fear them. They slashed, hacked, making the vampires bleed. Swarts came up to one who just killed three soldiers trying to tackle it, burying his axe in its neck. Its head flew off. Then he heard Major Dong scream, a vampire feeding on him, sucking out his blood. This one looked female, obsidian skinned, and she had a look of glee in her eyes. Swarts came in when something grabbed him as well, knocking the axe out of his hand. It was an ivory vampire, bald, his mouth covered in blood, Swarts not knowing that this was the vampire that had started all of this death.

Swarts drew a knife and stabbed him in the side. The creature screamed in pain, but it grabbed Swarts' neck, and the last thing that the Colonel heard was a horrible cracking sound and his own life going black. Orson looked around. Lee-Arne joined him. The battle was ending. It was short, quick, but ten vampires were also lost. There was also a smell of fuel in the air. He didn't like it. He called as the remaining twenty soldiers were surrounded by ten vampires. They got one of his kind bringing their numbers down to twenty. But the rest were killed or fed upon within thirty seconds.

When it was done, the vampires came to Orson, who pointed to five of them and said, "Check for survivors then join us."

They nodded, searching the dead while Orson and the remains of the clan joined him. He had sent three others to search for the second group of soldiers tonight, hoping that this threat to the knowledge of their existence would be contained. Once the three he sent out to find the remaining soldiers in the woods returned, they would head to Northern Canada. There was a small clan up there, but as long as they stayed out of that clan's hunting range, it'd be alright.

Chaplin Wright heard the cries of battle outside, and though it only lasted four minutes, it seemed to last forever. When the last battle cries were silent, Wright knew what had happened. He sent a prayer to heaven, asking God to care for the fallen souls of the soldiers. When done, he took the lighter, and put it to a stake that had been drenched in diesel and mow gas, a rag wrapped around it. It blazed to life, and he waited. The flap of his tent opened and five of the vampires came in, wearing sunglasses to shield their eyes, the Chaplin looking at them. Four ivory, one obsidian, all looking excited at this final meal.

Then they noticed the smell. The smell they had noticed outside the tent, that of fuel, and noticed how strong it was in here. Wright smiled and said, "Too hell you go, you demons."

He dropped the torch, it hitting the ground, lighting him and the remaining vampires on fire. Wright didn't scream as he burned with them, hoping only God would save his soul and burn these demons.

The smell of flames hit Orson and the fourteen remaining vampires with him, and he turned, putting on sunglasses to shield his eyes, seeing the camp ignited on fire. The flames spread making a symbol. The symbol was a circle, a cross in it, the ends reached the circle's edge. Vampires were not repelled by symbols of religions, but the message was clear. We repel you. He also knew the five he sent in were burned as well.

He turned, the others staring in horror. He sighed and said, "Head back to the cave, grab your coffins. We will wait for the remaining three."

"We should help them," said one of the remaining vampires.

Orson shook his head. "Stick to the plan."

They nodded, but as they zipped off, Orson could sense something else in their movement: fear. They were afraid they had gone too far, and another clan would soon be wiped out.

***

Jenny saw them under the cover of the bushes; she and the remnants of 514 were under the bush. Three vampires: two obsidians, one ivory; they stood there, their fangs and claw hands seeming to glow in the night, sniffing, looking for their victims. Jenny had a flare in one hand, and an axe in reach of the other.

The vampires turned to the bushes, Jenny's heart pounded, Hamish, next to her, went pale.

"Come on Hickman, please," she prayed. They started walking slowly to them. Ten seconds passed, twenty, thirty. She could almost smell the earth on them as they got closer.

The sounds of shots fired broke the silence of the darkness, and the three turned, screaming their terrible cry, and rushed to the sound of the gunfire. Then Jenny, Hamish, Garcia, Jackson, Sosa and ten others stood, the vampires turned away from them, looking for the source of the noise, and the soldiers lit their flares.

The new sound made the three turn then cover their eyes, screaming in the night. One blindly turned, its claws grabbing at a tree, and it scurried up it, reminding Jenny of a Kong Fu movie where a ninja just seemed to fly up a tree. Jenny charged at the other two blinded vampires, flare and axe in hand, 40 soldiers behind them. The vampires tried to flee, but to their flanks, five soldiers on each side of them stood, their weapons hot, firing rounds and keeping the two immobilized, screaming and bleeding. Hickman was leading them.

Garcia and Jenny were the first to reach them and swung, axes in hand, swinging at their neck. They hit and the bullets stopped firing, black blood coming out of the two. Behind them, ten more soldiers charged in, stakes in hand, and impaling the two creatures in their chest, bursting their hearts. They fell down, dead.

A cheer wrenched in the night, but Lt. Perry said, "We got one more. Get ready."

Everyone raised their weapons, the forest canopy pure dark, unable to get their target. But they heard the rustling in the treetops. It was moving around up there, moving like a spider monkey, hidden in the shadows of the canopy.

"Where is that bastard?" growled Hickman, he and Hamish back to back. Jenny and Garcia were doing the same, as was Jackson and Sosa.

A scream came out, PFC Kim, who was near the rear of the group, went flying up, a claw hand in her belly, the creature going back up the tree, the short Taiwanese girl dropping her rifle, trying to free herself. They all froze, and the screams continued until they were stopped by a horrible slurping noise. Then a body fell out of the darkness, like an angel falling from heaven, landing among the soldiers, Kim's throat torn open.

A cackle reached them, and it said, "Come on little pigs. Come and try to catch me. I will drink you, one by one. Seventy-nine, 78; who is going to be seventy-seven? Any volunteers? That is what you people do, isn't it? You volunteer for death for the betterment of your people. Come now. I don't want to be kept waiting."

"Come down and face us you coward!" yelled Jenny, her anger eclipsing her fear, her axe almost sings in her hand, wanting to dismember this vampire.

Another cackle. "None of you are a match for me, little pig. No human can match me."

"I've killed three of your kind!" Jenny yelled.

"I've slain one of you demons as well," roared Hamish, "I cut its head off."

"Killed one of you tonight as well!" yelled Garcia.

"And I," said Hickman, who paused, then, slightly embarrassed said, "Well, I found a way to trap you."

"You lie," said the thing in the trees, but a note of doubt now entered his voice, and Jenny thought she could sense its fear. They were breaking it.

"Come down here you coward!" yelled Lt. Perry. "Face your

death like a man."

Thud. The vampire landed in the middle of the remaining soldiers and screamed, "I am more than a man, little pigs."

This was what Lt. Perry feared. It landed in the middle of the group, where it was strongest, able to use its speed and strength to its full advantage, the soldiers too clustered to risk using their rifles. It slashed down ten before they could react.

However, the night before, this creature had the advantage due to the company being unprepared for the attack. Tonight, they knew what they were facing. The vampire killed another four before it was tackled by ten soldiers, pinning it, and it using its claws to kill four more, but was pinned when more soldiers joined the dog pile. Soon it was pinned under a few dead and many live bodies. Lt. Perry and SFC Alibudbun charged in, axes and stakes in hand. Perry reached the pile first, and he raised his axe, the blade singing, and it went through the creatures open mouth. The blade broke its fangs, and went through muscle and bone, the top of its head was removed.

It stopped struggling, going dead instantly. The soldiers got off it. Twenty were dead, but tonight, though they didn't know it at the time, 18 vampires were killed. Wasting no time, they grabbed their gear, quickly prayed for their dead in many different forms, and took the final push to Malone.

CHAPTER FOURTEEN

Aftermath

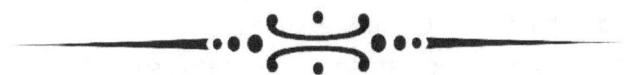

"Nevertheless, life and death are mysterious states, and we

know little of the resources of either."

— Joseph Sheridan Le Fanu, *Carmilla*

Officer Dean had been lost for hours. His GPS wasn't working on these dirt roads. He had no cell signal. Only the radio was working. Twice he had to turn around. At 1712, in the darkness, Patrisha called him up.

"You make it, honey?"

Dean picked up the radio and answered, "Not yet, it's like a fucking maze in here. Why aren't the roads marked?"

"Security, I guess. Don't want us civilians crawling around out there."

Dean shook his head. And he thought the roads in Belaphone, Michigan were bad. Still, Malone proved to be a good change in venue. After the craziness of what happened in Leon County, he just wanted a change. He left after the Fair Creek incident and Belaphone was half burned to the ground by...by those things...no, no, don't think about that. That was behind him. This was fresh start; a new start. Twenty-three-year-old African Americans didn't get many of those, even those who were cops. Fucking white America.

He took another left, and drove down this road, were the trees seemed to be lighter, the road more clearly defined. Quarter mile down, he saw a sign. It was a federal warning to stay off this road. On the top it said, "Site Indigo."

"Patrisha, I think I found it. Going in."

"Okay," answered Patrisha, "be careful, sugar."

"I will."

He drove down, feeling nervous. Then he smelled something, something like…it was smoke. Black smoke, being blown north. His stomach dropped. He quickly picked up the radio.

"Patrisha," said Dean, "I got smoke. Call the fire department. Might be a forest fire."

"Copy."

He drove further and soon saw the origins of the smoke. It was the camp and it was ruined. Trees surrounded the outside. Remains of trucks and debris from equipment laid scattered around them. Dead, the dead bodies, hundreds of them, just lying there, glowing in his headlights, fully armored and armed. They were all mauled, slashed, and bloody. Some looked drained. He drove to the south side of the camp downwind of the smoke and got out of his cruiser. The camp showed evidence of being wider, but had condensed itself into a small, fortified area, where the flames were located. A wall of fire. The smell of burning corpses were mixing with the smell of death; almost making Dean throw up the meatball sub he had eaten earlier. The cop went to his knees, dry heaving. After a minute, he got to his feet, and his stomach still churning, but then saw what looked like a cargo container with a generator at the end.

He walked there, almost against his will, suspecting but needing to confirm what was in there. He felt the temperature rise as he got closer to the flames. He reached the container, saw the handle, pulled it out and opened the container. In the glow of the fire, he saw more dead, over two hundred, these looking older, crammed in, and all also bloody and mauled. He turned away, resisting the urge to puke again and ran back to his patrol cruiser. He got in and grabbed the radio.

"Patrisha," he said, his voice cracking.

"Hang on, honey, two soldiers from Fort Drum just...

"Patrisha, they're dead."

On the other side of the radio, Patrisha saw the two soldiers walking in as Dean called her. Knowing they would want information, she said, "Hang on, honey, two soldiers from Fort Drum just..."

She and the two who just walked in heard Dean's next words. "Patrisha they're dead."

Everything froze for moment. When no answer came, Dean continued, "Something got them, hard. There are bodies here. They look like a bear or something mauled them. They seemed to have lit the remaining camp on fire. It hasn't spread yet. Get every fire department in the area out here and call the state police. I need back up."

Before Patrisha could answer, Lt. Miranda rushed forward, "Are there any survivors."

"Who is this?"

"Lt. Miranda, I need to know what is going on out there."

SSG Carter looked like he was dazed, hit by a truck. Dead, how could they all be dead?

"It's just as I sa... stand by, got a chopper coming in, military."

The radio went dead, and Miranda started cursing and crying, and Patrisha seeing this, along with three other cops in the building, came over and hugged the woman.

Carter pulled out his own phone and began to dial Captain Choi.

Officer Dean saw the chopper, its green paint job glowing in the flames. Going to his trunk, he pulled out a flare as it circled, lighting it, and waving the sparkler over his head. The Blackhawk, seeing this, came in for a landing. It landed thirty feet away from Dean, its engines roaring in the night, the wind from the blades beating at Dean, who ducked slightly as it came down. As it landed and shut down, its side door opened, and four soldiers came out. Dean held the flare, its flame dying slowly as a PFC, two SPC, and a Staff Sergeant came forward. Seeing it was a cop, they lowered their M4s and came up.

"What happened?!" yelled the female SSG, her name tag on her IOTV showing her name was Rictard.

"Not sure yet," said Dean. "Just got here, myself."

"Any survivors?!" yelled Rictard over the dying chopper.

"No, it doesn't look like it. I know this is your jurisdiction, but we need to put out that fire. I'm having the fire department and state troopers come to handle the situation."

"Understood," said Rictard who nodded. "Don't worry about jurisdiction right now."

"Okay, who is your commanding officer?"

"Chief Warrant Officer 3 Gaddy."

"I need him, got a Lieutenant at Malone PD."

She nodded, yelled at the PFC, the kid running back to the chopper. A minute later, the Warrant Officer came out, wearing a flight suite and a flight helmet.

"Officer," said Gaddy, shaking Dean's hand for a brief moment.

"Come with me please."

Gaddy followed Dean to his patrol car and got on the horn as soon as the Blackhawk had silenced itself. When he could hear his own thoughts, Dean spoke, "Patrisha, did you get everything out of the stables?"

She answered as soon as he released the button.

"You got three different fire departments sending trucks. Also, about twenty state troopers. They are going to meet up with Lt. Miranda and SSG Carter here and they will bring them straight to Site Indigo."

"Good, is that officer still with you?"

"Yes, sir."

"I got Warrant Officer Gaddy here. Can you put the officer on?"

"She's on her way."

Dean handed Gaddy the mic, and he spoke into it.

"Chief Gaddy speaking."

"Chief," said the female voice of Lt. Miranda, oddly cool, "Radio up to Fort Drum. We need CID, MPs, and choppers in the skies. Until they're there, coordinate with local law enforcement to contain the fire. Once done, CID takes over the investigation, though we need local law enforcement to help. Colonel Norris and General McCoy will be coming later as well, along with Captain Choi from the 549."

"Yes, ma'am. As soon as we get it called up, we will hit the skies again. We will keep locals apprised of the fire if it spreads further. It's weird looking, a cross in a circle or something, like it was planned."

"Understood. Also, see if we can find any survivors. Any notes, journals, anything to find out what happened out there."

"Yes ma'am. Anything else?"

"That will be all."

Gaddy handed Dean the radio back, but there was nothing more to be said, and he put the radio back on its holder in the car. Gaddy went back on his chopper, the ground team staying behind, and took off, keeping an eye on the still contained but large fire.

Norris heard Captain Choi's phone ring and saw him pick it up. She and General McCoy drove back to the 549 after General Bryant's breakdown, him being sent to Samaritan Medical Center in Watertown. They were still in shock, even more so when SSG Carter called in from Malone.

Choi, seeing this, turned on the speakerphone so the General and Colonel could hear.

"Sergeant, what is it?"

"They...ahh, sir, the report just came. As of 1745, it's reported that it appears there are no survivors of the 549 field mission. Hundreds of dead were found, some in the refrigeration unit, others just left where they were, and over a hundred burned. Damaged vehicles and equipment was found and secured by the team from the Blackhawk sent out. There is also a report of fire, so local fire departments and law enforcement is being dispatched to Site Indigo who will be escorted by me and Lt. Miranda."

The silence that followed was almost a physical thing. It hit General McCoy, Colonel Norris, Captain Choi, and SGM Curry like a punch to the gut. Things like this are expected from war, but not here, not at home where they were supposed to be safe. How this happened would never be fully known, save for little knowledge gleamed from the lucky survivors that would be found later. But as for right now, there was nothing that could be done.

"Thank you, Sergeant," said Choi finally finding his voice,

speaking almost robotically, "Please coordinate with local law enforcement and wait for CID and MPs to arrive on site."

"Yes, sir."

The line was cut, and they all sat, their expressions too horrible, disbelief and fear, as there was only one way to explain what they had done. They failed, they failed to act when they should have acted, and now, it was over. They had failed the men and women of the 549.

General McCoy finally spoke, tears in his eyes for the third time that day. He had lost more soldiers than any other person in there put together, and he knew what all of them were feeling, even though he had never knew any of the members of the 549 until today.

"Call FRG and let them know to coordinate with the Red Cross. I'll contact the Pentagon to apprise them of the situation. Contact the Chaplin Corp as well here on Fort Drum. There are going to be a lot of funerals in the upcoming weeks."

They all nodded.

"Captain Choi, recall all on rear guard and have them outside the Battalion in an hour. We have to make the announcement. Look up all next of kin so when we have identified the bodies, we can contact them."

Choi nodded, told Curry to make it happen, and the NCO left.

General McCoy turned to Colonel Norris and said, "We got some calls to make."

They left. DOD was going to be having a nightmare in a few hours.

At 1845, the 49 soldiers on rear guard for the 549 support battalion were assembled. Most were in civilians, having gone home for the day, and told they didn't need to change back into OCPs. They stood there in one confused semi-circle, wondering what was going on. When Captain Choi, Colonel Norris, and General McCoy came out, Curry ordered them all to attention. They fell in. Curry saluted the Captain and said, "All present and accounted for, sir."

Choi stepped forward and said, "You all know Brigade Commander Norris. You might not know Lt. General McCoy. He is from the pentagon, originally just passing through, but he has some things to explain to you."

He stepped out of the way, leaving the soldiers confused. But the tall General stepped forward, a look of sorrow on his face and said, "Sorry for the recall, but, I feel this should come from me not because I'm part of your chain of command, but because you need to understand what is happening, and how it would affect you and your love ones. So please, I will make this quick, but listen carefully."

The soldiers were silent; scared something was going to keep them up all night.

"As of 1745 today, all soldiers in the field mission at Site Indigo, code name, ECP Forward, are confirmed dead or MIA."

There was a whispering, a mix of gasps and confusion that the General allowed to happen, letting them process what was going on. After a bit, the General said, "Settle down."

They did, and fearful looks stared back at the General. He couldn't blame them. McCoy took a deep breath and said, "This means, as of this current moment, the 549 is no longer an active component in the United States Military. The Battalion is basically gone. Even if a hundred survivors were found, it wouldn't be enough to rebuild the Battalion. DOD is considering reallocation of the Battalion's resources at this time as well. This why as of this time, and this including Staff duty, I'm sending all of you home until further notice. You are going to be worried about your friends and loved ones in the Battalions, and I can't blame you for it. I believe three of you are married to soldiers that are still out there and unaccounted. I am not going to subject you to Army bull until we get some more information. All I ask is that you do not share what happened over social media until the press conference I am planning tomorrow. We are going to hope there are survivors and go from there. As soon as we have more information, we will put it out to you as quickly as possible. Some of you may, later on, be sent out to other units in Fort Drum, and maybe some other bases. But until that happens, do what you have to, whether it be prayer, drink, sleep, or whatever, to help yourself get through this. But do it safely and don't make a bad situation worse."

The soldiers stood there, and McCoy saw a few tears in their eyes. But he finished with, "Stay strong, stay motivated, and hope for the best. Have a good night, and don't come to work tomorrow. MPs will be handling guarding the equipment here until further notice."

The soldiers, the NCOs, and then one or two officers there walked away, a feeling of hopelessness on their shoulders. McCoy, now alone with the senior officers, for the only time that day, let himself cry.

At 1930 hours, CID agents arrived on the scene of Site Indigo, and the place was controlled chaos. Fire fighters were putting out the flames of the burning camp, the blackened metal, burned canvas of a couple of tents, and the blackened remains of over a hundred dead soldiers. They never found evidence of the creature, their bodies having been turned to ash by the flames, nor were they looking for any sort of supernatural explanation, only of that which was in their own limited scope of belief that was true reality. The problem being that scope, when it came to crime, was usually right. Humans killing humans, the remains of a more supernatural existence, if there even was one, had never once entered the Army detective's thoughts, for such thoughts were long thought to belong to that of our ancestor's superstitions, and long discarded by modern man and his unwavering belief that science had all the answers.

Two Chinooks had arrived earlier, a space cleared for them to land. The Army personnel, fifty, spilled from the two choppers, assisted the civilian cops and firefighters. Later, twenty-five LMTVs and ten Navistar 7000s were dispatched to the site, not for rescue efforts but recovery. Bodies some burned but the rest showing evidence of being mauled to death by something. Maybe animal attacks. The CID agents put this forward as a likely answer. Problem was, though limited, they did have live ammo. Army regulations prohibited using weapons for killing local wildlife, but when it came down to it, better to kill one or two bears than let them kill a few soldiers.

General McCoy, Captain Choi, and Colonel Norris came in at 2000 hours, met up with Lt. Miranda and SSG Carter, who had led the firefighters and State Troopers in over three hours ago. They came up with CID Agent Littlebear, a Cherokee soldier and a top-notch CID agent. They stood there, the three new arrivals seeing what had happened. They had witnessed 911's aftermath and wars that followed, seeing scenes like this was not an uncommon site. But here in America, not since the Civil War, had something like this been seen on mainland America.

"How many?" asked Captain Choi, his stomach doing roller coasters in his belly.

"Seven hundred fifteen bodies found so far," said Littlebear, "Some were mauled to death. Others seemed to have been drained of their blood. There was evidence of live shots being fired in that direction."

Littlebear pointed over to the ring of trees, his finger directly opposite direction of the camp.

Norris looked up, a slight bit of hope in her cheeks.

"Seven hundred fifteen, that means there are still 134 bodies still not accounted for."

"We're looking for them, and some record of what happened here," said Littlebear, "but there is nothing yet. We got search parties looking for more bodies."

Norris wiped at her eyes, McCoy patting her back. Unknown to any of them, a fireman, under the pretext of getting coffee, handed his hose to another fire fighter, the flames almost gone. He walked away from the site and found an area clear of men. His hands going under his thick, yellow coat, he pulled out the green journal he had found in the remains of one of 549's trucks. He opened it. It was the journal of Colonel Swarts, and giving it a quick view, he got the gist of what happened. He pulled out his phone and dialed a number. It was answered on the first ring and the man spoke in quick Italian.

"Un clan è andato troppo oltre. Chiama i cacciatori. Dobbiamo sapere cosa è successo."

There was a quick acknowledgement. "Inteso." Then the line went dead. The firefighter put the journal back under his heavy coat and headed back to the camp. He did what needed to be done; now he could go back to helping his temporary allies, for the dead would need to be put to proper rest.

"Hey," said Hamish, "look over there."

Four miles outside of Malone, they found hard top pavement and the 59 remaining soldiers, haggard and warn, felt a little hope. Help was close. A car even passed them, but though all 59 waved them down, the then unknown to them drunk driver just gave them the finger. So, when Hamish called on something, even Jenny felt like killing him for interrupting their march to salvation. But then she saw it. In the forest on right side of the road, several trees looked like they were knocked down. It looked like something big and heavy was dragged into it.

Lt. Perry called a halt and said, "Dang, Garcia, Hamish, Hickman, you all with me. Sergeant Alibudbun, continue leading the rest to Malone."

"Yes, sir. Let's go."

The five remaining soldiers started walking to the hole in the tree line. It didn't go in far, and hidden in the dark branches, lighted by flashlights thanks to Jenny and Hickman, they saw it. It was a HEMMIT, a large cargo truck used by the US Army, painted green, a flat rack, covered by a green tarp, and lying on its driver side. It was the ammo truck, almost forgotten. They went forward. Driver and passenger were inside, shown through cracked front windows. They were dead. The passenger hung via a seat belt, suspended over the driver. Hickman went around to the back, the rest staring at their dead comrades.

Jenny, using the trucks construction, climbed on it, and managed to open the passenger side door that was open at the top. It was heavy, but she managed it. She looked inside. Both men were mauled, and the radio was slashed.

"Vampires got them," she said, climbing back down.

"Must have followed it," muttered Garcia, as she's holding Hamish's hand, who was praying for the men.

"Hey, some good news," Hickman came back, carrying a box of ammo. "Ammo still there."

"We will have to secure it later," said Perry, "But for now, grab two boxes. Fill your packs with the ammo inside. We might still need them."

They did, and then ran back to the marching soldiers.

Officer Gillals saw the group about a half mile down the road, he himself, perched on a small off-road path, hidden by the hill he was on.

"What the fuck?" he said, thinking they were some kind of protest group. That was until he saw the green uniforms and rifles. Fucking paramilitary.

He got on the radio, "Patrisha, looks like some paramilitary group is marching into Malone. Going into..."

His cellphone rang then, and he checked the number. To his surprise, it was Patrisha.

"What the..." he answered.

"Gillals," she almost yelled, "go down there, and see if they are from the 549 support battalion."

"What?"

"Do it and don't hang up."

Shrugging, he drove down, his headlights on, and he drove down to see what the fuss was about. He parked ahead of them, leaving the lights on and the siren off. He got out of his car, and in the lights of the cruiser, he saw them, at least 59 soldiers, all covered in bloody uniforms, many of them bleeding and injured. They stood there, staring at the cop with a flicker of hope in their eyes.

"Uhhhhh, you guys with... ummm, 549?" asked Gillals slowly.

A young Lieutenant at the head of the group confirmed this. Patrisha got the confirmation from Gillals, who said, as if teary, "We are sending help now. See if any needs medical assistance."

She hung up.

"What the hell did I miss?" asked Gillals to nobody in particular.

A Vietnamese looking girl laughed and said, "So much."

Lt. Miranda got the call about two minutes later. She was over by bodies, helping with identification when she got it. She answered, and two seconds later ran to Colonel Norris, who was with General McCoy and yelled, "Ma'am, they found 59 survivors in Malone, 59 from the 514 MSC!"

Norris and McCoy looked up. Their jaws dropped, their eyes widening. Captain Choi, who had overheard, ran up and asked, "Are you certain?"

"Yes," she said, "they got Lt. Perry's DOD number, and were able to confirm it."

"Let's get to Malone," said the General.

"Sir, they mentioned that there are 60 dead. They are in the woods across twenty miles, northwest of here."

"I'll handle that," said Choi. "Lieutenant, join the Colonel and General, get to Malone."

She did.

CHAPTER FIFTEEN

The Revelation

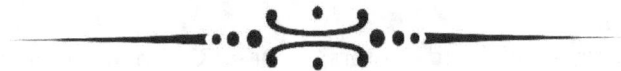

"What is life, in the end, but a series of small victories and larger

failures?"

— Guillermo del Toro and Chuck Hogan, *The Fall*

Orson ran ahead of his pack. It was past midnight. It takes another two hours to get back to the cave in Black River. He felt full but also knew his leadership was eroded. He had lost over twenty of his kind to mere humans, twenty. How? How did these humans not feel fear? How did they not fear him?

Lee-Arne stopped, her obsidian frame suddenly frozen in the night. Orson skidded to a halt and ran back. He asked her, "What is wrong?"

"They are not back yet," said Lee-Arne, staring out in the moon light.

"They will come when they are done."

"They should have been done over two hours ago."

Orson hissed, and said, "We don't have time. We need to get back to the nest."

Lee-Arne turned back to Orson and said, "We lost five last night. Legwang is gone, and now, there is only fifteen of our clan left. If the humans killed the other three, we have to kill them, tonight; full force."

Orson was about to yell when the others came out of nowhere, surrounding the two, looks of anger and fear of discovery on their faces.

"We went too far," said Cain. "They will send hunters after us now."

"They won't send hunters," snarled Orson. He looked back towards where they left, and said, "They seemed to be heading to the town where we hit the truck."

He looked at the time, 2039. It takes a few hours to get back to where they were at, but there will be plenty of nighttime left to get back to the cave. He looked up at Lee-Arne though, she's looking hungrily to the northwest. She had challenged his authority. She had trapped him in a situation and forced his hand. She had planned for this. What else was she planning in that devious little mind of hers? He didn't know, but he was going to keep a better eye on that obsidian little bitch. If worse came to worse, his fangs would taste vampire flesh tonight. He saw how Cain, Maguri, and the rest zipped with her now. This situation was soon going to have to be dealt with, and very soon.

***

The survivors of the 549 were brought to Malone's own Red Roof Inn on 42 Finney Boulevard. General McCoy paid for them personally as he and Colonel Norris, driving in Lt. Miranda's car, paid for via his personal, vast, bank account. He paid for fourteen rooms. They were filled, though First Squad, of Third Platoon, chose to all stay together. Six crammed in, Garcia looking her tired and harden troops with relief and pride.

Jenny sat there with Hickman, they, like the others not dealing with masks. Fuck coronavirus. If they could handle three nights of attacks, and win, they could do anything.

"It's over," sighed Hickman. He had brought a bottle of Jack Daniels he had bought at the gas station not too far away. He had also bought three packs of Kool menthol. He was a happy son of a bitch.

Sosa and Jackson were snoring on the floor. Garcia took the time they slept to sit on Hamish's lap, kissing him, not caring if she was caught. Jenny, however, axe at her side, was oddly quiet, as she stared out of the window. The news of the 549, being all but destroyed, was still haunting her mind. Survivors guilt she guessed. But no, that wasn't it. There was something else. Something heavy was weighing on her mind. Maybe it was supposition, or paranoia, but she felt it wasn't over, not tonight.

"What's wrong, Jenny?" asked Hickman, Garcia and Hamish still too busy cuddling to notice them talking, Hickman taking a swig. "We made it. We survived."

"How many others survived?" she asked. "Did anyone ask?"

"We'll find out," said Hickman. "Bet you they kicked ass."

There was a snort of laugher as Garcia touched Hamish's side, making him react with laugher, surprisingly, not waking up Jackson or Sosa.

"Come on, man," said Garcia, her voice adding a twang to her beauty, her smile bright, all enhanced by the fact she was finally able to take a shower and brush her teeth. God: showers. Jenny smiled remembering it. And brushing her teeth, god that was a blessing. Still, Madam Roseta saw her now; she would have scolded Jenny for, as she would put it: *not caring for how you look. How are you to be a star if you don't pay attention to yourself?*

A knock on the door made them all jump, Jenny, instinctually, grabbing for her axe. Then she remembered, those things always came unannounced, and wouldn't care about a mere door in their way.

Separating from Hamish, Garcia walked to the door, looked through the peep hole, and opened it. It was SFC Alibudbun. He said, "Grab your weapons and form up."

"Awe…" groaned Hickman, "I just opened the bottle. Now it's going to lose it new booze smell."

Jenny and the rest of first Squad followed downstairs, and when they passed the front desk, she saw how nervous the front receptionist looked. She couldn't blame her. Dozens of haggard looking soldiers armed with carbines, axes, stakes, and flares. She looked like she was nearly to the point of losing her mind.

They assembled, and Jenny realized how small they truly were. Third Platoon had nearly lost half its members. From 40 to twenty. And they were the lucky ones. Forth platoon had only 15 members left. Second, also 15; first nine. They were all that was left, and Lt. Perry stood before them, a sad look in his eyes.

"I just got a call from Colonel Norris." he said, slowly. "Other than rear guard and us, the 549 has been all but wiped out. We are all that is left."

Jenny's heart sank. She felt sick. No, it couldn't be.

"A General McCoy is coming to check on us, and we will be air lifted back to Fort Drum. There are decisions that have to be made, and what is left of our equipment will have to be recovered, but, as for us…well."

Jenny was going to raise a hand to wipe away tears, and she wasn't the only one. All of First Squad, her entire platoon, the remnants of her company, cries came out into the night, a sense of failure on them. They failed to save their comrades in arms.

Then Jenny had a thought and it sent a nearly nauseated realization up her spine, and she looked over at Hickman,

Hamish, and Garcia. Even Jackson and Sosa were looking like they were just punched in the stomach.

"They are covering their tracks," moaned Jenny.

Everyone caught that, even Lt. Perry, who looked up and said, "SPC Dang, I'm..."

"Those creatures, they were meant to kill us tonight," she continued. Then even Perry got it.

"They tracked us all through the forest." moaned Hickman. "Somehow they always knew where to find us."

"They are going to come here, to Malone," gasped Garcia.

The company, for a short time, sorrowful, was now looking like they were scared puppies, realizing they had just exposed over 14,000 people to the horror they just encountered.

Ten minutes out from Malone, General McCoy's cell began to ring. He pulled it out. Instead of a number, it showed a message. Priority. Confused, General McCoy answered.

"Yes?"

"General McCoy," said a voice in what sounded like a thick, Romanian accent, "Please do not hang up. If you want your surviving soldiers to survive the night, you need to listen to me very carefully."

The General felt anger, and Norris and Miranda noticed this.

"Is this a threat?" he snarled.

"No." the voice was emotionless, not reacting to McCoy's anger, "It is a warning from a friend. The creatures that attacked your battalion over the past few nights, they will not want any witnesses, of their existence, to remain alive. They are going to go and clean up their mess. They're going to Malone."

"Creatures?" asked McCoy. "Who are you?"

"I am one of the few who has all the answers to what happened to the 549, which I cannot give at this time. And I am taking a risk telling you this. The organization I belong to has known of these creatures for quite some time and track their movements. There are barely over a hundred left, but this type of incursion, it is a highly unusual behavior for them. It has been decades since they've risked such attacks."

McCoy's mouth dropped, not sure whether this was a crank call or real, but if there was a chance what this Romanian sounding man was saying was true, then he had to get as much info as he could.

"What do you suggest?"

"How many men can you get from Fort Drum to Malone in less than two hours?"

"I can't send men to occupy an American city without Presidential orders..."

"Listen to me General, what is about to occur tonight goes beyond little things like paperwork or orders. These things are going to kill all who witnessed them, even if that means the streets of Malone run red tonight with blood."

"If you're so sure, why can't you send help?"

"My people could never get to Malone in time. But I tell you this, General, because they can be stopped. This is not a goal of my organization. These creatures, though they may feed on the edges of humanity, they are both intelligent, and endangered. We try to keep them contained, and until now, we managed it. But this clan is desperate and will try and keep their secret. A secret that everyday gets harder to keep as technology advances. They are difficult to kill. However, it's not impossible, and they do have weaknesses, but you will not have time to collect them all tonight. Destroying their heart or beheading is the surest way to kill them. Axes and blades are surer than bullets. Bullets can't kill them, but it takes either a hell of a lot of them, or very big ones, but they can hurt them. Explosives will be more effective. They are sensitive to bright light, flares being effective at blinding them. Fire also harms them. Sunlight as well. As for silver and garlic, you won't have time to collect such things tonight."

"Silver, garlic, what are we fighting, vampires?" laughed McCoy.

"I can neither confirm nor deny that," the Romanian flat tones were so clear, McCoy stopped laughing. What was going on?

"I was sent to track a clan that had just settled out here about two weeks ago. I arrived four days ago myself. The clan was forty-two strong. Do you hear me now and realize the threat? Forty-two of these beings took out over 700 of your men in three nights. They planned for this, using General Bryant as their unwitting puppet."

"How do you know General Bryant? How did you get my number?"

"My organization is well connected. We have cells in all corners where these creatures travel, ensuring that attacks like these don't happen. But I dropped the ball. By the time I realized what was happening, it was too late to act. Now, I have a chance to make up for my mistake."

"If they are so strong, how are my guys going to be able to stop them?"

"There were strong indications at the site that several of these creatures were killed. Ash shadows on the grass, I counted at least twelve and five more in the forest, tell-tale signs that they were killed. Whether alive or dead, their bodies disintegrate in the daytime, only leaving behind ash. Your men are going to be facing between 15 or 20 of these creatures. Again, a dangerous number, but it is possible to save lives tonight. By the way, I'm sending you the locations of your fallen men. I found them deep in the forest."

There was a buzzing on McCoy's phone and a picture of a map appeared in McCoy's text message. He opened it. A picture of Google maps came up, and two markers appeared on it, south of Malone.

"How do you know where they are? Wait, you were there tonight?"

"Yes, I helped with the fire, which, I do not say lightly, was the very least I could do to atone for my mistake. Send men to Malone tonight, General. Hopefully nothing happens. But if I am right, lives will be saved tonight."

The line went dead, and General McCoy was silent, until Colonel Norris' phone rang. She answered and looked up at the General.

"Sir, that was Lt. Perry, he says he suspects..."

"I know," said the General, almost automatically, barely aware of the words spoken from his lips, "Is Colonel Anderson still up?"

"Should be."

The General called.

"Colonel Anderson."

"Colonel, how many men, armed to the teeth, can you send to Malone in an hour?"

"Sir?"

"How many can you cram on a couple of Chinooks?"

Anderson was silent for a long minute, then, "Ah, about two hundred sir, why..."

"Load them up now."

"Yes, sir, they will be ready in an hour."

"Get them a hell of a lot of ammo."

He hung up, turned to Miranda and he said, "Step on it."

Miranda nodded, and speed down the last bit of road to get to the Red Roof Inn.

Lt. Perry, SFC Alibudbun, Sergeant Garcia, SPC Dang, Hamish, Hickman, PFC Sosa and Jackson all stood outside the Red Roof Inn, the remaining members of the 514 were rearmed with axes, pickaxes, rifles, tent stakes and some flares. They looked tired, unshaven, barely awake, and yet ready for combat.

A car pulled up, and three occupants got out in front of the eight who were waiting for them. General McCoy, Colonel Norris, and Lt. Miranda came out.

The eight fell to attention, and they saluted the assembled officers. General McCoy returned the salute, came to Perry and said, "I just got the strangest call in my life telling me the 549 Support Company was basically wiped out by vampires. So, is this a hoax or was the call I got true."

"Sir," said Perry, "I say it's true."

The General nodded. "Okay, so, can you confirm how to kill them?"

Perry quickly summarized the ways they killed the five that attacked them and the heavy toll it took on his men. Norris and Miranda were confused, but the General nodded and asked, "You sure they are coming back tonight? And who are these guys?"

Perry responded, "I am sure, sir. And this is First Squad of Third Platoon. They have racked up all but one of the vampires we killed. SPC Dang here has killed three herself."

The General looked at her, and asked, "You willing to fight tonight?"

"Yes, sir," responded Jenny.

The General nodded. Then he called, "Manager, stop harassing those soldiers and get over here."

The manager, a young Polynesian woman in a professional suite and black mask came over and said, "Sir, I have other people in the hotel who are getting nervous. Now I have allowed your men to keep their weapons, understanding what they been through, but this is going..."

"Call your police chief," he said. "Then if you have his or her number, call the mayor, and tell them to get over here in twenty minutes."

"Sir?"

"Malone's in danger and I'm going to be breaking many laws to protect it. Evacuate the hotel tonight."

"Sir, I can't."

"Do it."

She scampered, compelled to obey. Then McCoy turned to Norris and said, "We've got work to do."

***

Legwang found what he was looking for that night. He had only enough time last night to break the gas line that blocked the soldier's main path to Malone, but it was only a stopgap. He hoped Orson would finish up soon. He would have a great surprise waiting for him.

The large coffin was stuck in the branches of the fallen trees of the Black River, ten miles away from the cave, bound by silver and he would be unable to break it. Carefully, he walked into the river, making sure not to go over his head less he drowned himself, and pulled the coffin out of the water. He heard the banging inside, though it was weak, the Elder having gone three nights without feeding.

Pulling it to the shore, dragging it on land, the vampire

punched at the wooden top, smashing the coffin. The Elder was there, his body looking more like a corpse then the great vampire Elder it once was, and it stared at Legwang, who was surprised no water got into it.

"Legwang," said the Elder weakly, "help me."

Legwang had a sorrowful look on his face as he pulled the Elder up from the coffin into a sitting position, and said, "I am sorry Elder, but I must act for survival of the clan."

"No," moaned the Elder, but it was too late, Legwang's fangs biting into the Elder's neck, draining him of blood. The Elder's blood tasted vile, but it surged into Legwang like fire, he's feeling the power of the Elder entering into him. When he was finished, the Elder's body looked like a husk, nothing but dried skin and bone.

He dropped the dead Elder into the coffin, then grabbed a flare he stole from the camp the night before he left the clan, covered his eyes, lit it, and threw it in the coffin. The flames consumed the Elder's body in seconds, turning it and the coffin to ash. The cursed earth added to the fire, the flames purging unhallowed ground.

Legwang smiled. Now, he was the true Elder.

CHAPTER SIXTEEN

The Battle of Malone

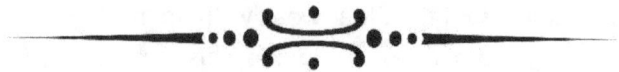

"He thought, in fine, that the dreams of poets were the realities
of life."

— John William Polidori, *The Vampyre: A Tale*

The mayor drove up and saw the 63 soldiers going in and out of his hometown Red Roof Inn. The Mayor was a short, stout, crazy gray-haired man with glasses, in a tweed suite that gave the impression he was a professor of science from a prestigious university. However, he was in fact a retired car salesman, who ran for mayor just to escape the sheer boredom. Being Mayor of Malone was a comfortable and fulfilling job for one Mayor Atlee. Malone, and its 14,000 residents, provided a full day of challenges while at the same time was small enough not to be too overwhelmed. But right now, this frazzled looking man was marching forward, chest puffed up, his police chief, and a man who looked like a Caucasian gorilla, marching at his side with four other cops.

The police chief, in the middle of the night, about 10:00 pm, had awakened Mayor Atlee. He said that a General McCoy had summoned him. Initially, Atlee refused but the chief insisted, saying the General was claiming there was danger to Malone. Atlee lost his cool.

"Of course there is danger for Malone. In case you haven't noticed, we are in the middle of a fucking pandemic. The General can wait."

Despite looking like a simian to Atlee, Chief Keys was actually a calm and firm man who had many more brain cells than Atlee, and as a former Marine, managed to convince him that a 3 Star General's warning was worth listening to. So, grumpy but convinced, he put on his suite, and marched out into the cool autumn night, picked up by his chief of police, and headed to the Red Roof Inn.

Marching up the streets of his town, he found the General standing with Jenny. Jenny, though looking nervous, was asked by McCoy to help him explain the situation. He asked her because she had marked up the most kills of the things, those, well vampires, that had wiped out the other companies of the 549. She had also confirmed many of the ways to kill these things that were explained by the mystery Romanian sounding caller that had contacted him. He looked around, wondering if the Romanian was still here, watching in the background. He didn't like the idea he was being observed by an outside force, but he had a feeling he was going to need to listen to him.

The Mayor and his cop posse came up, and Jenny was impressed that this little man who looked like a mad scientist was looking up at the General with coldness. If she did such a thing, she would have paid for it. "Perks of civilian life," she muttered under her breath, her lips barely moving.

"General McCoy," said Atlee, "I only agreed to meet you tonight in the middle of a fucking pandemic because my chief of police here has convinced me that it would be unwise to ignore a warning from a US Army officer. But I have to remind you I am under no obligation to obey any orders that are given to me by you unless directed to by the Governor of New York or by Federal order. Soldiers do not have the authority to commandeer a hotel for a command base and declare Marshall Law without Federal orders. However, you have proceeded to do so. I want to know why so I can know exactly what to say in the letter I'm going to send to the Governor."

McCoy listened and Jenny noticed how coldly he looked down at the man. But he let him say his peace and said, "If you're done Mayor, I will explain. Yes, I usually can't send soldiers, even when I know a city is about to be attacked. I have to send that information over civilian channels and let them handle such threats. That is why I need your direct permission to send in a few hundred men to secure this area. It's in a gray area of the law, hell, probably against the law, but a threat is coming here to Malone."

He then indicated Jenny, "This is SPC Dang. She and the 59 soldiers are all that is left of an attack that happened in Site Indigo outside of Malone. I have lost 790 soldiers over a course of three nights, basically an entire battalion, to a force of 41 rouge elements that mauled my men to death."

"Mauled," said Chief Keys. "You mean…"

"The 549 support battalion was engaged in hostile actions against these unknown combatants, but we do know this: none of them were killed by bullets. They were either slashed to death or their throats were ripped out. Tonight, the field mission had a final stand, and this was the results."

He pulled out his cell phone, bringing up pictures of the base camp, formally known as ECP Forward. He handed the phone to Chief Keys, who strolled through them, Atlee watching. The more they watched, the sicker they looked.

"My god," said Atlee.

"I do know that a few of these unknown combatants were killed. However, I have reason to believe that they are going to try and cover their tracks. That means, killing those who survived the massacre."

"Then you should get them back to Fort Drum," pointed out Chief Keys. "If what you said is true, your putting Malone citizens at unwarranted risk."

McCoy took back his phone, swiped across it, and brought up a new picture. This one of the overturned HEMMIT. He showed it to both the Mayor and Chief.

"That's why. We have reason to suspect that these creatures would be more then capable of attacking us on the road. We do that, we put more civilians at risk, and not just those from Malone."

The Chief and Mayor looked at each other, and the Mayor said, "You're putting my people in danger now, just being here. Play your war games somewhere else, and just..."

The General was suddenly in his face. The Chief tried to move between them, but the General held out a hand, and Chief Keys' old instincts of obeying officers kicked in and he surrendered.

"These things are coming tonight. We are not leaving. So, you go ahead and write that letter to the Governor, I don't care. But if we can stop them tonight, we will."

The Mayor was stunned, but the Chief believed him and said, "What do you need, sir?"

The General turned to him, grateful for an ally.

"How many officers do you have?"

"Thirteen."

"Stay out of the fighting, but there is a truck full of ammo out there. If your men can secure it for now, I got a lot of Army officers coming and can collect it later."

"Yes, sir, what else?"

"Chief," said Atlee, indignant, "you work for me."

"Shut up," snapped the chief, and the mayor, surprised went silent, "What else sir?"

The General looked at Jenny who asked, "You got any flares?"

"Yeah, a lot," said Keys.

Jenny saw Lt. Perry passing behind them, and she turned and said, "Sir, on that ammo truck, other than bullets, was their anything else being transported on it?"

Perry paused, thinking, the realization came to his face. "You know, I think there were some grenades on it."

"Grenades?!" yelled Atlee, his eyes bulging.

"The launching kind or the throwing kind?" asked McCoy.

"Both. We don't have launchers but..."

"We have two," said Keys. "Army surplus M320s. We use them to launch tear gas canister."

"That will work."

"Chief," said the General, "any grenades you find on the truck, send to us. Another box of M4 rounds as well. You remember those?"

"Yes, sir," Keys pulled out a cellphone, and started to make some calls, the Mayor walked away, looking angry.

General McCoy looked at Jenny, who looked worried, and said, "I hope nothing happens tonight, but if it does, you might want to consider putting a retirement packet together."

"Let's hope we can survive the night," said Jenny, a cold chill going down her spine. She walked away. McCoy hadn't battled these things before, and as he watched her walk away, he sent a prayer to God that he would survive this coming fight.

First Squad stood together in the chilly night, Jenny with her axe in hand, a tent stake with her as well. A combat knife hung from her belt. Hamish was armed as well, his dullish, Army axe replaced by a sharper fire axe from the now abandoned hotel. Sergeant Garcia and Sosa also were armed with tent stakes and axes, too. Jackson and Hickman were armed with their rifles, four full mags in their pockets. On a bandoleer over Hickman's left shoulder and across his chest, several grenades, both launch and throwing, and was walking around with the biggest grin on his face.

"Three years in the Army," he said. "First time I felt like Rambo."

"Hopefully, your last as well," said Garcia with a smile.

"Hopefully, our last night of attacks," said Hamish, looking at the clock. It was 0100 hours, and barricade was made. Mattresses, desks, even a couch from the hotel. All the while, the manager threating lawsuits as the soldiers commandeered the furniture with Chief Keys assisting with quick warrants that would not hold up in court later. What they were doing was violating laws that were federal, and risking their necks to protect small town America, going against thousands of pages of US legislation on this very subject. They all knew they could wake up tomorrow and be sent to Leavenworth, but that didn't matter. What mattered was tonight, they were going to need to stop these things.

Garcia stood, and looked at her remaining squad and said, "Whatever happens, I am proud of you guys."

Jenny and the others smiled at first, but then Jenny stood, and saluted the NCO, something you don't do unless reporting, but Jenny had too much respect for her. She stood and honored this brave NCO who stuck with them no matter what, despite of her relationship with Hamish. Hamish, Hickman, Sosa, and Jackson all stood as well, and saluted the NCO, honoring her with their respect. She may have broken a code, but despite this, she made damn sure they came out alive. The bandage on her hand, from the cut she gave herself to save Hickman and Jenny attested to that. She fought to make sure they would all live, and not just her husband.

Seeing the salute, SFC Alibudbun came over and asked, "You realize she's not an officer, right?"

"No," said Jenny, "she is our leader."

Alibudbun nodded and said, "Nice job with the picket line. Doubt it will be enough."

"It doesn't matter," said Hickman. "We got other advantages, other than new bombs."

"Oh," asked Jenny, "such as."

"We have more people, and we know how to kill them," said Hickman with a smile.

"There were 849 of us before this happened," said Hamish, "now we are down to 59."

"I still like our odds," said Hickman, "Still say we should have gotten some garlic and silver if we could."

"We don't know if that's even true," pointed out Garcia, "Hell, until a few days ago, I thought vampires were a myth."

"Makes you wonder what else is out there," said Jenny as Colonel Norris and General McCoy came up.

"Building evacuated?" asked Norris.

"Yes, ma'am," said SFC Alibudbun.

"Good."

"What about Site Indigo?" asked Jenny, first time ever speaking candidly to an officer.

"Well," said McCoy, "they're still collecting bodies, but I

don't think they are at risk. If my gut is true, then I don't think these things will be going back there tonight. They're going to want you."

"We'll see," said Hamish to himself.

Before anyone could respond to this pronouncement, Lt. Miranda came up and said, "Choppers are 10 minutes out, ma'am. They have the quadrants for the landing zone."

"Good," said McCoy. "Let's hope we won't."

"We got vamps. Fifteen, I count fifteen."

The call came from SPC Cortes, and without question, the soldier, including First Squad grabbed their weapons and prepared for the fight of their lives.

Jenny came up, axe in one hand, flare in the other, her stake on the ground. They were there, about a 500 feet down the road, outside the pool of electrical light. Eight ivory, seven obsidian vampires, looking hungry and... desperate. Yeah, that was it, desperate. Jenny saw that. She saw tonight that they were not leaving until all who witnessed them were dead, no matter the price.

Good, she thought, *because I'm going to kill every last one of you for what you did to my battalion.*

The rest of First Squad joined her. Hickman grabbed his M320 launcher along with Davis, a second platoon survivor, and they took aim.

"Let them have it!" yelled Perry. Hickman and Davis were more than happy to oblige. With loud, hollow sounds, the two launched the grenades at the creature, who, realizing what was happening, scattered. One didn't get so lucky, an ivory one behind the rest, and before he could zip way, Hickman's grenade hit between his feet, and exploded the ivory vampire. It went flying, its body ripped by shrapnel, one of its arms flying off, its clothing on fire, landing a hundred feet away.

"Woo hoo!" yelled Hickman. "Got that son of a bitch."

The other vampires came back, looking at their fallen brother, and Hickman and Davis were about to take another shot when what they saw made them freeze. The vampire stood back up, its arm gone, but its body sealing wounds that would had killed a human, including a twisted leg, which reset itself.

"Oh, shit," said Hickman, "No, I didn't. No, I didn't. No, I didn't!"

General McCoy came up, just as shocked as the rest, for the first time witnessing the power of these things, but yelled, "We knew this wasn't going to be easy. Ten minutes people. All I want those reinforcements to do is clean up after us."

"Hooah!" yelled the soldiers.

"Fall back!" yelled Perry. "You all know the plan, make them come to us."

The soldiers fell back from the barricade, Third Platoon First Squad standing together, and ready to fight the monsters who rushed forward, fangs exposed, ready to fight. Jenny and Hamish raised their flares as the 61 soldiers assembled into smaller groups, ready to fight.

The vampires charged. The armless one, the one that Hickman hit, seemed to teleport in front of First Squad, its remaining claw wanting to rip apart Hickman for what he had done to him. But Jenny and Hamish lighted their flares before it could do anything, blinding its black eyes.

The one armed vampire screamed: his arm flung out, hitting Jackson in the head, breaking his neck and sending him flying. Jenny ducked, swung her axe, and buried it into the creature's chest. Sosa darted behind it and swung her own pickaxe into its skull. The creature flailed for one more minute then died, its body collapsing.

Sosa was about to go get Jackson's weapon when an obsidian vampire came up from behind, sinking his fangs into her neck.

"No!" yelled Garcia, grabbing her knife, and buried it into the creature's neck, the blade coming out the other side, black blood oozing out. The creature, unable to scream, sent Sosa flying, dead from blood loss, and then punched Garcia in the chest, sending her flying. She landed on the grass on the other side of the road.

"Camila!" yelled Hamish rushing to her as Hickman and Jenny went at the creature. It tried to run, but Hickman shot at it with his grenade launcher, hitting it in the chest. The projectile went through, burying itself in the vampire's chest, and Jenny had to fling herself and Hickman down, the grenade exploding the vampire from the inside, ripping its body into a thousand pieces. Jenny looked up and saw Hamish picking up Sergeant Garcia, taking her behind a parked car, protective of her. Jenny and Hickman ran to them. Hamish was holding her, and it seemed that Sergeant Garcia was having trouble breathing. The sounds of battle seemed to get far away, Jenny watching Hamish hold his secret wife, seeing how much the loved each other.

Then Garcia's eyes open and she said quietly, "I'm okay baby," she weakly touched Hamish's cheek, a tear going down the ex-Amish's face. Then she looked at the rest of her soldiers and said, "Get back in there, that's an order."

"I'm not," said Hamish.

"Go," said Garcia. "I'll be fine here, baby. Keep as many of us alive as possible."

Jenny put a hand on Hamish, who looked up, nodded and gently hid Garcia under the car, Hickman keeping guard. When done, the three charged back.

It was getting bad. Half the remaining soldier of the 514 were fighting, the rest dead or too injured to keep going. But about five vampires, including the two First Squad took down were dead as well, and each vampire killed gave the remaining fighters hope. Jenny, Hamish, and Hickman charged in, ready for a fight. One vampire was feeding on Cortez, he long dead, and Hickman took another shot at the vampire, who went flying, landing on the barrier, and was set upon by five soldiers one missing a hand, impaling its heart with tent stakes, the wood sticking out of it like a pincushion with oversized needles.

Another was killed by Lt. Miranda, stabbing it in the heart when its back was turned. Three vampires saw this and charged at her, grabbing her, and Jenny knew they were trying to tear her apart.

"No!" she screamed.

"Jenny, wait!" yelled Hickman but it was too late.

Jenny ran ahead, grabbing a flare, charging at the three vampires and their screaming victim. At ten feet, she yelled, "Hey!"

They looked up, and Jenny lighted the flare. They screamed, dropping Miranda, her left arm and right leg were dislocated but she was alive. Axe in hand, and picking up a fallen tent stake, an arm falling off it and charged the vampires. The first she reached was an obsidian one with an afro. She ducked its flailing arms and stabbed it in the chest with her tent stake. It fell, its heart popped like a pimple. Feeding on adrenaline, she rushed the second one, her axe swinging through its neck, its head flying off, landing ten feet away. The third swung at her but she managed to dodge its blind blow and buried her axe in its shoulder. It screamed in pain, and Jenny, drawing a knife from her belt, jumped on it, stabbed it in the neck and as she did so, landed on top of it while twisting the knife that separated the neck from the rest of the spinal column. She stood, and pulled out the axe, with Hickman and Hamish joining her.

"Damn, girl," said Hickman, looking at the three dead vampires, making the number of vampires only six, but only 12 tired soldiers left to fight them. The three turned to help but then something hit Jenny from behind, breaking her left leg and sending her tumbling into the road, her hands and chin getting scraped as she landed. Hamish turned to the bald, pointed ear, ivory vampire, and swung his axe, but the vampire grabbed it by the handle, pulling Hamish in then punching him so hard he flew back twenty feet; several of his ribs were broken.

Hickman managed to shoot at it twice, but it then zipped behind him, grabbing his right shoulder with a clawed hand, and breaking the bones underneath at the same time the two projectiles exploded on a parked hatchback. Hickman screamed, driven to his knees, in too much pain to do anything. The creature then went to Jenny, Hickman and Hamish unable to help, bones broken and in too much pain to think about anything else. He looked at Jenny, who was trying to crawl away from him, but he flipped her over, and landed on top of her and said, "I'm impressed, human, but I can't let you live after you killed my brothers and sisters."

Jenny screamed in defiance, pushing back against the creature's shoulders, watching the creature open its jaws, revealing sharp teeth, like that of a small shark. Torturing her with fear, it slowly lowered its head to bite her neck. She pushed back but she was no match for the creature. She could feel something scrape against the skin of her neck. Then there was a light. For a moment, Jenny thought she was going to heaven, swearing she saw an angel in the light. A humanoid form, with wings, she swore was in the beams. But the loud sound of a Chinook Helicopter engine disproved that, the twin rotors buffing the air, creating strong winds that even took the remaining vampires by surprise. The vampire turned and saw the two choppers coming in for a landing. He turned back to Jenny, screaming in rage.

The choppers landed and two-hundred rangers came running out, rifles ready, and the surviving soldiers, which there were not many, cheered as they charged in, squads coming in via V formations, firing at the six remaining creatures, including the one that had broken Jenny's leg. Jenny watched as bullets took chunks from it that healed quickly before he could zip away. Three others, realizing that they would die if they continued fighting, zipped away as well, but the remaining two didn't have a chance and were mowed down, the bodies unable to escape the hail of bullets keeping them from moving. Lt. Perry then charged in with Colonel Norris, who lost an ear, and they swung their axes, the reinforcements seeing this, stopped shooting as the two remaining vampires were beheaded.

Medics from the choppers went to Hamish, Hickman, Garcia, and Jenny. They went to the other survivors as well. There were not many. At the end of the battle, of the 61 soldiers that fought the vampires, only nine were alive. General McCoy, Colonel Norris, and Lt. Miranda survived, injured and alive. And of the 514, only six survived. This included the remains of First Squad, Lt. Perry, who lost an eye, and SFC Alibudbun, whose legs were broken.

CHAPTER SEVENTEEN

The Hunters Awaken

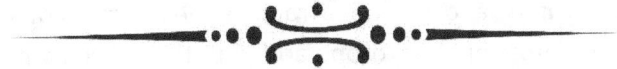

"I decided as long as I'm going to hell, I might as well do it
thoroughly."

— Stephenie Meyer, *Twilight*

Deep under Saint Peter's Basilica is the location of the Necropolis,
around 5 to 12 meter depending on where you stand in it. But
beneath that was another chamber, leading down to about
another 17 meters, where one would find a steel door. This
door's existence is unknown to all but the current Pope and his
most senior staff members and the commander of the Swiss
Guard. If you put your hand on the hand scanner, and it does not
recognize you, the chamber will fill with aerosol poison, killing
the intruder. It will seal them in with another steel door that
would kill you and stop the poison from getting into the
Necropolis above. For Monica Rossellini, this was never a danger
for her. When she put her hand on the scanner, the door opened,
and let her into a blue-lighted room, metal walls and stone kept
this chamber undetectable.

Monica didn't work for the Vatican, in fact she tried to avoid
the priest and cardinals that live in Vatican City as often as she
could. But she had the pass that allowed her to enter all levels of
the Vatican, one of only three women, and it was not a public

thing. The ones above, tried to save souls. Those who worked below, tried to keep an eye on the things that feed on those souls.

Monica walked in, her long black hair going down to her waist, her curved and attractive frame made one think of a movie star. The professional wardrobe added to that effect: a business jacket and a skirt. But Monica was no actor.

She got to the room she needed and opened the door. Inside sat a Chinese man of seventy, Mako Lang, and an African woman from Kenya, Lupita Maina, who was forty-five. If one was looking at these people, they'd assume them to be business partners, not warriors. But they were warriors, and more importantly, watchers.

"What was this incursion?" asked Mako, his thick accent making it hard for him to speak as clearly as he would like, but he got his message across.

"The clan our agent was tracking went rogue," said Monica, "They attacked a USA training mission for the US Army."

"Survivors?" asked Lupita, her beautiful features marked by concerned.

Monica said, "Nine. We have their names."

"The clan?" asked Mako.

"Four confirmed have escaped."

"Did the Elder sanction this attack?"

"No, our agent found his coffin, burned, and vampire ash found inside, along with the remains of silver and garlic."

"Was he drained?" asked Lupita, leaning back in her chair, crossing her legs.

"I suspect so."

"By the one of the four?" asked Mako, leaning forward.

"No, our agent suspects that a rouge vampire went against

the clan and drained the Elder himself."

None looked shocked or angry, but they were all worried about what was spoken.

"A new Elder has awakened. Are the other clans aware?"

"No, and they wouldn't have sanctioned such an attack. We have informed them via the usual way. A few will be meeting tonight in Iraq."

Mako nodded, "Good. Whoever this new Elder is, he will want to purge what is left of the old clan to make a new one. He will hunt the four."

"And they will be like beast," pointed out Lupita, "And attack any who gets in their way."

"Shall we awaken him?" asked Monica. "The hybrid?"

Mako looked at Lupita, who nodded and said, "He would be the best."

Mako took a deep breath, sighed and said, "Awaken the hybrid."

Monica nodded, stood, and started walking out of the chamber, down the hall, and into a second door with a hand scanner and retina reader on it. She lined up her eye and put her hand on the scanner. Both devices turned green and they opened the door for her, the flat metal sliding along its recesses, and disappearing into the wall.

The room looked like a hospital room, with a small Italian doctor inside, monitoring the thing in the bed. She walked over to the bed. An onyx figure was sleeping in it. The creature didn't have pointed ears or clawed hands, but his mouth did have two elongated fangs inside, but also regular human teeth as well. Monica knew when the creature opened its eyes, its eyes would be black as well. In its right arm, a catheter was inserted, connected to a line with a blood bag hanging from an IV pole. The short, Italian doctor joined Monica on the opposite side of the bed. Monica stared at the creature for a few more seconds, and without looking at the doctor, said, "Wake him up."

The doctor nodded, went to a cupboard, and pulled out a syringe filled with two cc's of Naloxone. He removed the line feeding blood to the creature, and inserted the needle, pressing the plunger. Within ten seconds, the creature took a deep breath, and opened its dark eyes. It turned its head and saw the doctor, then turned it head again, and saw Monica, and she did not miss the bulge that rose the sheet that covered his naked body.

He spoke in perfect Italian. "My beloved Monica, you haven't aged a day."

She smiled and kissed the creature on its lips. When done, she stood and said, "Liar, it's been five years since you were last awakened."

"Five years. Anything new?"

"Lot of things, but you know we don't awaken you unless it is necessary."

He nodded. "A rogue."

"Five we believe. There is a new Elder, and four clan members he will hunt down."

"Cause?"

"A clan went against its Elder and attacked a battalion of soldiers."

A look of disgust came over the creature's face. He sat up, his onyx skin giving him an eerie glow in the blue light, hard muscles under his flesh.

"They doomed themselves. Was it sanctioned?"

"No."

"The other clans?"

"We are waiting for their response."

The creature nodded and stood, the sheet falling off his body. He was completely hairless, but that was due to genetics, not choice. Monica looked at him up and down; smiling as she remembers the last time she had this man thing between her legs. He couldn't give her children, but love, oh, yes, he was good at that.

The Hybrid looked at her and said, "How is your daughter?"

"She's fine."

"I missed her, as I did you."

She blushed and smiled. The doctor came up, giving the hybrid his clothing. He changed, wearing an old hoodie and sweatpants.

Monica gave him another kiss and said, "Come, we have work to do. I missed you, Samer."

"I did as well."

The two left the room.

***

Orson, Lee-Arne, Cain, and Maguri all made it back to the cave two hours before sundown. They entered, the realization of what had happened still haunting them. The humans beat them, they beat them into retreat. Orson felt the others glaring at him as they went to their coffins, blaming him for what happened. That was until they saw what was before them. The coffins, all 41 of them, were destroyed, ripped apart, the earth scattered about. Orson's mouth dropped, fear hitting him like a battering ram.

"Had a good night?" said a cheery voice.

They turned, and in the dark cave saw Legwang standing

before them, a large smile on his face. His teenage like body looking relaxed, and well fed.

"Legwang, what have you done?" asked Orson, desperate, looking at this boy like creature, who looked like he was having the time of his life.

"That's Elder now," said Legwang with a smile. "I drank the Elder's blood. Show some respect."

The four looked shocked at this pronouncement, and fear hit Orson. He knew they only had one chance and said, "Will you take us in your clan?"

Legwang snickered, knowing he had Orson by the balls. He seemed to think about it seriously for a long moment, but then said, with a wide smile that revealed his fangs, "You are all so fucked."

Orson turned to Lee-Arne and said, "Grab dirt and run."

"Orson."

"Go."

Orson flew forward tackling the still laughing Legwang, who was cackling like a hyena even as Orson struck him.

Lee-Arne and the others dove for the dirt. They stuffed as much as they could into their sacks and ran out of the cave where the two vampires wrestled. They got outside, deciding on which way to go, when there was a wet thud. Lee-Arne turned. Orson's head laid on the ground, ripped from its body, which remained in the cave. From the cave, a laughing, cheerful voice said, "Run, little pigs, run. I'll hunt each of you down, and I'll have my fun. Then when I'm done, I will rebuild the clan."

The three ran as fast as they could, running west. They would be running for a long time, running from this crazed thing of an Elder that sat, laughing in the cave, looking forward to having their heads.

***

Jenny woke up in a drowsy sort of way. She was in a hospital; her mind being dulled by a morphine drip going into her arm. Her broken leg set in a cast and suspended over her bed in a sling. She looked around the room, and soon saw she wasn't alone. Hamish rested in the bed next to her, Sergeant Garcia in a wheelchair, holding his hand. His chest was wrapped in bandages to stop his chest from expanding too much. Hickman was in the bed next to him and his shoulder was heavily bandaged, his arm in a sling, but he looked like he was just enjoying the high from his morphine drip.

Jenny tried to sit up, but she was barely able to move the way her leg was positioned. The sound of her movement caught Sergeant Garcia's attention though, and she sat up, letting go of Hamish's hand and rolling to her.

"Dang," she said when she rolled to her, grabbing her hand.

"Sarg," Jenny said in a hoarse whisper, her throat felt dry. Garcia went over to a side table and got her a cup of water, helping her drink it. It helped. She was then able to speak easier.

"Are they okay?"

She indicated Hamish and Hickman.

"Hamish has five broken ribs but, he will be okay. Hickman's shoulder was crushed, but the doctors repaired it surprisingly well, considering."

"And you?" asked Jenny.

"I'm fine. Mostly bruising. One rib got busted but that was all. And found out that I might have a new mouth to feed in seven months."

Jenny's eyes widen. "Does Hamish know?"

"As soon as he is better."

"What about the…" Before Jenny could finish, there was a knock at the door. A nurse came in and saw her four patients. She was a blonde woman, who looked like she could belong on the cover of Playboy, but had the look of a caretaker on her face, and smiled kindly.

"How you all felling?" she asked.

"We're okay," said Sergeant Garcia. "Have you…"

"We contacted your families," said the nurse, "but there is someone here to see SPC Dang."

"Who?" asked Jenny.

"A Madam Roseta. You know her?"

Jenny smiled, "Send her in."

The nurse left, and Garcia looked at Jenny in confusion.

"She's my emergency contact."

Garcia smiled and the door opened again, and the Romanian dance teacher came over to Jenny, her eyes taking in Jenny's leg, and the bandages on her chin and hands.

"Oh my god," she said going over to Jenny. "Jenny, are you okay?"

Jenny nodded, "I'm okay, thanks for coming."

"Ooooooooo," said Hickman in the corner, his voice spurring due to the pain killers. "Mama, baby, am I seeing an angel?"

"Shut up Hickman," laughed Garcia, rolling back to Hamish, continuing to watch her secret husband.

Roseta pulled up a chair and sat next to Jenny, holding her hand and talking to her about new dance moves she would like her to try, also talking about her son and husband. It kept Jenny distracted from the nightmare of fangs that was playing in her head.

Another knock came from the door and it opened. A young doctor walked in, and Jenny thought he looked like Doctor Karev from *Grey's Anatomy*. Handsome but tough looking, with a good heart.

"Hey, came to check in."

"Scooby Dooby Doo, where are you," sang Hickman in a drunken singsong voice.

"Well, that one is feeling better," laughed the doctor and he went to Jenny.

"Hi," said Jenny, trying not to blush.

"Hi, Jenny, I was told you were awake. I'm Doctor Morrison. I was your surgeon."

Jenny blushed, flustered, knowing Madam Roseta would normally scold her for not looking her best, but the ballet master only stroked her arm, like how her mother used to when she was sick.

"Well, thought you should know we called your mom," said Morrison. "She and your father are on their way, but thought we should talk about the surgery you went through. Doubt you remember much; you were pretty out of it."

Jenny nodded, and even Garcia and Hickman looked up, curious. This caused Doctor Morrison to say, "Would you like to talk in private?"

"No," said Jenny, looking at the remains of Third Platoon and First Squad, "they're my family, too."

The doctor nodded and said, "Well, both bones in your lower legs, your tibia and fibula, were clean breaks. Cleanest I ever saw, in fact. We reset the bones with rods that we surgically inserted. A few months of relaxation and physical therapy should do the trick. There will be a little discomforted in your leg, but as long as you don't try any crazy hops, you should be fine."

The comment was not intended to make Jenny upset or had any intention of harm, but when the doctor's pronouncement was finished, tears welled up in Jenny's eyes, and her throat was unable to work, causing concern to pass over Doctor Morrison's face. Roseta, who also realized what this meant, grabbed Jenny's hand and put an arm around her shoulders, careful not to move her too much, but giving Jenny comfort.

The situation wasn't helped when the drunken voice of Hickman drifted over, saying, "What about her career as a ballerina?"

"Shut up, Hickman," snapped Garcia, who also realized what this meant for Roseta.

"I'm missing something here," said Doctor Morrison. "Am..."

"I'm a dancer," said Jenny. "I was going to go professional."

"Oh," said the Doctor, realizing his mistake, "I'm sorry, Jenny, but, with this type of leg injury, I don't know if it will ever heal enough to let you go back to dancing."

"No," said Roseta, "there has to be away."

"The type of surgery she would need would require a specialist in the field, and I don't believe the Army would cover that type of surgery. There are therapies we could try, but, still, it wasn't just the bone. There was some muscle and nerve damage as well. I hate to say it, but I don't know if your leg will ever be the same. I'm sorry, Jenny. I'll come back later."

The doctor left and that left Roseta and Garcia to comfort Jenny, her dreams shattered. Finally, she said, "I'm done. I joined up because of a dream. Now that dream is gone."

"Honey," said Roseta, "Don't give up. You still..."

"What's the point?!" screamed Jenny. "I'm done. I don't want this Army bull shit anymore. I want out!"

"Tears in the rain," muttered Hickman, quoting from *Blade Runner*.

"Hey," said Garcia, rolling back to her, "we'll figure it out.

We will."

"Jenny," said a hoarse voice. Everyone looked around. Hamish's eyes were open, in pain, but determined.

"Jacob," gasped Garcia, rolling back to him, "baby, you okay?"

He gave Garcia a warm smile. Then he looked over at Jenny again.

"Jenny," he said again, "we survived. As long as we have done that, we are good. We survived. We can try and rebuild ourselves from our experience."

Jenny wiped her tears away, a slight hope coming back to her. Hamish was right. As long as they were still alive, they had a chance to reclaim lost dreams, even though they are like tears in the rain at that moment, lost forever in time.

"Thanks, Hamish," said Jenny. Garcia was back to holding her husband's hand again. Roseta held Jenny.

Hickman muttered, "Who's gonna comfort me? Maybe I should call my mom."

They all laughed.

CHAPTER EIGHTEEN

Endings

"Love is so great... So why does it have to go so wrong?"
— Hideyuki Kikuchi, vampire Hunter D Volume 3: *Demon Deathchase*

General McCoy stood outside Carriage Area Hospital where the remnants of the 549 were being treated. He and Lt. Perry were the only ones not being treated, having only minor injuries. He looked out in the street, never before being so grateful to see sunlight. The dark of night now seemed like a cursed thing to him. It would always seem cursed.

A limo pulled up, and a Lieutenant got out of the car, his OCP's fresh and crisp, not having seen combat. He hopes they would always stay fresh. The Lieutenant went over to the passenger side of the rear of the Limo and opened it, indicating the General should get in. He did, feeling like there were stones in his stomach. He got in, and a Four Star General sat across from him. General Rhinheart, the chief of staff, and the highest-ranking officer in the US Army looked at him, his face set, not showing emotion. His brown hair was set in a high-top buzz cut, hard lines on his face looked almost carved. His dress blues, flawless. Lt. General McCoy hadn't expected this.

"Morning General," said Rhinheart with a thick southern

draw he got from Mississippi, his cold blue eyes staring.

"Sir," he said, "I didn't know..."

"I got the call last night, and the reports from the division Sergeant Major. Thought we should talk."

"Should I start putting in a retirement packet sir?"

"I recommend it," said Rhinheart, "You did occupy a town without presidential orders. Also, you did order other such units to land in a town and effectively making it a war zone on US soil."

"I did, sir."

"Half of Washington DC wants to string you up like a scarecrow. These actions don't look good on DOD. However, considering...something...killed 840 men on US soil, soldiers who volunteered to fight overseas, and somehow you managed to drive off last night, I managed to convince them to lower it to forced retirement and reduction of rank, to Major General.

McCoy smiled slightly. Not a happy smile. It was a smile of doing the right thing and being blamed for it.

"Still a good retirement package. Sir, were the combatants...ah...remains found?"

"Creepy things," snarled Rhinheart, "I saw the pictures. Unfortunately, we don't have them anymore. The Rangers who came to your rescue, along with the police department in Malone secured the sight until State troopers could take over. Unfortunately, that happened around sunrise, and the bodies...well...they are saying the enemy's remains caught fire."

McCoy nodded, Rhinheart noting how he looked unsurprised.

"And the four that escaped?"

"We are not pursuing," said Rhinheart, "Mostly because that is not our job. We're sending the info over to the Feds, see if they can figure out what you fought, but with the elections over, the old man being booted out, the Leon County incident, coronavirus, and this incident under his belt, Federal Government and agents are going nuts right now."

McCoy nodded. "Sir, I was unable to get a hold of Agent Littlebear this morning. Are they still at Site Indigo, and did they find a record left by Lt. Colonel Swarts?"

Rhinheart looked at him, thinking over the answered, but then said, "No, they didn't find anything. All that damaged equipment over there, well; they're still sifting through it. So far, nothing."

McCoy nodded, wondering if he should mention the Romanian who called him. He decided not to. Too much weird shit going on.

"They did find the bodies when they got that text with Google maps you sent. By the way, how did you find them?"

So much for that idea.

"I got a tip from a man. He sounded Romanian. He was the one that warned me about the attack coming from Malone."

Rhinheart raised an eyebrow, the first time showing any emotion.

"Can you get ahold of that man?"

"No, I tried."

He pulled out his cellphone and handed it to the General. He raised an eyebrow again, noting how it came up as just *priority*, no number attached.

"I have reasons to believe he was there at Site Indigo. I believe, though, he is long gone."

Rhinheart nodded.

"Well, too bad. Maybe he could shed some light on what happened."

He turned his head to the hospital and asked, "How are the

survivors?"

"Alive, but only myself, Lt. Perry, and Colonel Norris didn't need major surgery. The rest, well, I see a few medical discharges in their future."

Rhinheart nodded, "Long road for them. But, they are the lucky ones. Eight hundred-forty soldiers were dead. This is the largest amount of American soldiers lost on the US mainland since the Civil War, and worse, we can't tell their families the reason why they're dead."

"Sir, what about the equipment?"

"What's left of it at Site Indigo, we're getting civilian contractors to move it. Going to cost a fortune, but it has to be done. The weapons are being secured by the MPs and being sent to 549 arms room as of now."

"Will the unit be rebuilt?"

"Afraid not. The remaining soldiers will be placed with new units, and what's left of its equipment will be rolled out where it is needed."

Rhinheart looked out, his eyes were distant. He then looked at McCoy. "Any of those guys trying to stay in?"

"Colonel Norris, Lt. Perry, and Sergeant Garcia have indicated they will, however, the others, SPC Dang, Hamish, and Hickman, I doubt."

"Expedite the paper for early release. What equipment they left out there, just write it off as field losses. Put in the paperwork for full medical for all of them. They deserve it."

"Yes, sir," said McCoy, glad he would be able to help. "Also, sir, what about General Bryant?"

Rhinheart shook his head. "They're throwing the book at him. It was through his actions and inactions that 840 soldiers are dead. I'm sorry, but there is nothing we can do for him."

McCoy took a breath, "Sir, I know it's not my place, but I have reason to believe he wasn't acting on his own will."

Rhinheart shrugged. "It will be taken into consideration. Right now, he is in NYS Psychiatric Institute. See what happens. I know he is your friend, but he is responsible."

McCoy nodded, "May I tell his wife, sir?"

Rhinheart nodded.

"Sir, one final question."

"Make it quick."

"Sir, will Colonel Norris..."

"I suggest she retire as well. She may have only obeyed his orders, but sometimes you got to go against them. Lt. Perry and Sergeant Garcia will continue freely if they wish."

"Yes, sir."

"That will be all."

McCoy left the car and headed upstairs. Better start that packet.

Five months later

The soldiers were buried, the letters were written, the calls made, the tears flowed, and the reports were still being filed, but for First Squad, it was over.

Jenny walked out of Clark Hall, her DD 214 in hand, her car packed, ready to head out. Hamish and Hickman were right behind her. They had been reassigned to the aviation division. They had helped expedite their ETS leaves. Garcia was by Hamish's pickup. She had recovered and the Army had reassigned her to Fort Knox. She was already on PCS leave and Hamish would join her for the long drive there, her belly sticking out. When the coronavirus ended, he would start medical school.

He was also going to be closer to his brother and would try and visit him. His family hadn't come to see him in the hospital, they're still shunning him.

Hickman's dad was also there, picking up his son and driving him back to New York City. He looked nervous, but Garcia helped him feel comfortable.

Jenny's parents had offered to pick up Jenny as well, but she told them she wasn't going to be heading home. They were disappointed but knew that she needed space.

As they reached the parking lot, all four soldiers looked at each other, realizing that they were last of First Squad, Third Platoon. SFC Alibudbun had been reassigned to Clark Hall, waiting on early retirement and medical discharge paperwork, still in a wheelchair, unable to walk. Lt. Perry had left for Colorado, being promoted to Captain, and assigned as a company leader. They were the last. When they were gone, the 549 and the horrors they faced would be gone from Fort Drum.

They all had to relive the horror via Army investigation, and that memory was fresh in their minds. The vampires forever remembered by them. They looked at the world with new eyes. A darker, more mysterious world. It frightens them. Now they were facing the world again, only the VA for support when they were gone.

"Well," said Jenny, "I guess this is it."

Hamish nodded, "Try and keep in touch."

"I'll try," said Jenny, smiling but felling twinges from her leg.

"Same," said Hickman, his arm in a sling. The doctors did their best, but the damage was too severe, and Hickman's arm would never fully function again. He could still play guitar, but not as well as he once did.

"Lay off the beer," said Garcia with a teasing smile.

"Hey, helps with the pain," grinned Hickman.

His father, Patrick came up and said, "I'll take care of Tone. Make sure he doesn't get into trouble."

"Thanks, dad," said Hickman, with slight sarcasm.

They smiled, then came together, embracing in a group hug. Patrick walked back to the car, knowing his son needed this moment.

They broke apart. Then Garcia looked at Jenny and asked, "Still set on Michigan?"

"Yeah," said Jenny, "Got a friend in Traverse City. She already lined up a job for me."

"You could still join us," Hamish pointed out.

"Or come with me or my dad to Queens."

She shook her head, "Nah, I'll be fine."

They nodded, and they left for their vehicles. It was time to go. Jenny got in and took a moment to watch her friends drive off. She looked down at her DD 214 and realized she was free. She looked up at Clark Hall, and new she would never come back here or to New York ever again. She started up her vehicle and drove off into the sunlight. She came to love the day light, and was nervous every night, thinking those things would find her. Those vampires. Her hand gripped the steering wheel, and she looked down at her leg, realizing how much those things took away from her. Fuck them. If she ever saw one of those things again, she'd take back everything they took from her.

Putting the car in drive, she left Fort Drum, and drove to Even Mills, and stopped at Madam Roseta to say goodbye. She had been waiting for Jenny, taking her into her house and out crisp March air, and offering her coffee. They sat at the table, and Roseta asked, "Your leg doing better?"

A week before her discharge, she tried to dance, but was still having trouble, still, it showed that there was still hope for her dream.

"A little," said Jenny, trying but failing to smile.

Roseta came over and gave her a hug, saying, "You will see that stage and you will dance again; I know it."

"Thanks."

When they broke apart, Roseta said, "I will keep your portfolio on standby. Let us hope you will need it soon."

"I hope so, too."

A frown then came to Roseta's face, making Jenny worried for a second until she said, "Did they find those, ah, things that attacked you."

While Jenny was told by the CID agents not to tell anyone what happened to the 549 under UCMJ, Roseta was an exception for Jenny, as she always kept her confidence. The fact that her father may have told the truth about vampires had shocked Roseta, but she told nobody of Jenny's horror. Jenny shook her head, "No, but I didn't expect them to."

"You thinking about hunting them?"

Jenny laughed, "What, you think I going to take on vampire hunting?"

"From what I know, you killed six of them."

Jenny shook her head, "That was different. I never want to see those things again. If they come, well, I'll have an axe nearby."

They chatted a while longer, but Jenny knew she should get going. She stood, and the two hugged each other one last time, and Jenny left, her leg still sore but now able to walk normally on it. Jenny started her car, and headed down the road, heading west to Michigan.

EPILOGUE

Deep in the desert of Iraq, there is cave in between two large mountains. In the cave, down below, about twenty meters, it leads to a large, smooth chamber. What caused this cave is unknown, but it served a purpose. In the light of four high powered flashlights, The Hybrid, Samer, and next to him, his beloved Monica, along with Mako stood tall in the cave, their shadows cast like giants on the wall. Samer's onyx body was now covered by a black hoodie, the hood pulled up, combat pants, and black boots. Monica wore a similar outfit, Mako, who was too old to fight anymore, a simple suit and tie.

On the other side, just outside the ring of light were three beings. One was tall, black cloak covering his whole body, appearing wraith like, only his ivory hands and claws were revealed. The second was ivory as well, wearing a duster, plain shirt, slacks and shoes. Save for his pointed ears, fangs and black eyes, he looked surprisingly like a cowboy. It was the third who truly looked like a being from another age and time. She was obsidian, wore a thin, white dress made of transparent linen, and her golden head dress and the ornate adornment around her shoulders and covering the top of the dress, she looked like an ancient Egyptian queen. She had been one in life, but it was taken away when an Elder took her as part of his clan, but she in exchange took his life and blood, making her the elder. At 5000 years of age, she was not the eldest of the Elders, but being a ruler of both men and the undead, she was one of the most respected. Her beauty, even with those pointed ears, dark eyes, and fangs, was striking. She had no hair, but she did wear a black wig that formed her well.

The one in the cloak spoke first, his voice sounded like death in this echoing cave.

"What has your investigation revealed?"

Samer spoke; his more human features and still red blood contrasted with the beings before him, they seeing him as an abomination, but respected him as a hunter. This was not a hunt tonight. This was a peaceful interaction, and exchange of information, and hopefully, a simple agreement. The hunters did not kill vampires unless they go rouge. The recognition of their ancient knowledge and the history they held in their minds was too valuable to just kill off, the fact they had to feed on humans was not enough to let such knowledge go to waste, victims of the nature of their existence, and also a recognition of they, too, being sentient beings. As long as they and their clans stuck to the agreements, they would not be hunted anymore as they had to be.

"We have determined that the incident in Malone was caused by a rouge vampire, who turned against the elder. The Elder was bound by garlic and silver and sent down a river. One of his clans returned, and we believe sucked his blood, becoming a new Elder."

The queen-like vampire spoke, "Then why has this new Elder not revealed himself?"

Mako spoke then, showing no fear from these ancient beings.

"We think he is hunting down the last three members of his clan. Evidence shown over the past five months was that these three have split up; they were trying to hide it. As you know, our network in the Americas is poor, and regions population makes it hard to find the undead. I believe he plans to kill them before revealing himself."

The three understood. More than once they had to purge their own clans when they started to turn against the Elder.

"The Twelfth made his clan too large, too out of control. He was too selfish in his action." said the Elder in the duster, "It's surprising that he didn't purge his clan sooner."

The Queen spoke then, "Who do you believe is the new Elder?"

"We aren't sure."

"There was only one in his clan that I truly feared becoming an Elder," said the wraith.

"Legwang," said the Queen in a deathly pronouncement, "It is him. He is one of the few vampires older than some Elders. If he drank the blood..."

"He would dangerous indeed," said the wraith.

"He knows the agreement better than anyone," said the cowboy. "He wouldn't go against it."

"Don't be so sure. If he wasn't planning something, would he not have revealed himself?"

"Will you interfere with our hunt?" asked Samer.

The three looked at each other, as if conferring with telepathy. The Queen spoke for all of them.

"We will not."

"May we search with you, for Legwang?" asked the wraith.

The hunters already knew the answer to that. Monica spoke for them, "Is there another Elder in America?"

"Yes," said the cowboy, "The Seventh Clan is in Northern Canada."

"Will he send someone to hunt with the hybrid?" asked

Monica.

"Yes."

"We are agreed."

As if teleporting, the three disappeared into the Iraq night to rejoin their clans, and Samer looked at the other two and said, "I'll also need human hunters."

Mako said, "Too many clans in this region. I can send Monica and a few others with you."

"What about in America?" asked Samer. "Are there none?"

From out of a bag by Monica's feet she pulled out a file and handed it to him.

"Not a professional, but this girl killed six on her own. She is a survivor of the massacre."

Samer opened the file. Inside was a picture of a Vietnamese American, and the name, SPC Jenny Dang.

Samer nodded and then the three hunters left. They had work to do.

www.ingramcontent.com/pod-product-compliance
Lightning Source LLC
Chambersburg PA
CBHW060318260626
47160CB00007B/2653